playing

⋙ → *with* ← ⋘

matches

Suri Rosen

ecw press

Published by ECW Press
2120 Queen Street East, Suite 200, Toronto, Ontario, Canada M4E 1E2
416-694-3348 / info@ecwpress.com

Library and Archives Canada Cataloguing in Publication

Rosen, Suri, author
Playing with matches: a novel / Suri Rosen.

ISBN 978-1-77041-182-1
Also issued as 978-1-77090-594-8 (pdf) and 978-1-77090-593-1 (epub)

I. Title.

PS8635.O6495P53 2014   jC813'.6   C2014-902545-9
C2014-902546-7

Cover design: Jessica Sullivan
Cover photograph: © anas tonish/Photocase
Type: Rachel Ironstone

Purchase the print edition
and receive the eBook free!
For details, go to
ecwpress.com/eBook

The publication of *Playing with Matches* has been generously supported by the Canada Council for the Arts, which last year invested $157 million to bring the arts to Canadians throughout the country. We acknowledge the support of the Ontario Arts Council (OAC), an agency of the Government of Ontario, which last year funded 1,793 individual artists and 1,076 organizations in 232 communities across Ontario, for a total of $52.1 million. We also acknowledge the financial support of the Government of Canada through the Canada Book Fund for our publishing activities, and the contribution of the Government of Ontario through the Ontario Book Publishing Tax Credit and the Ontario Media Development Corporation.

Canada Council
for the Arts

Conseil des Arts
du Canada

ONTARIO ARTS COUNCIL
CONSEIL DES ARTS DE L'ONTARIO

an Ontario government agency
un organisme du gouvernement de l'Ontario

Canada

Ontario

Ontario Media Development
Corporation

Printed and bound in Canada by Marquis   3   4   5

RECYCLED
Paper made from
recycled material

FSC® C103567

For the Wineberg sisters
Fay and Molly

chapter 1

≫⟶ Hope and Inspiration for the Single Soul ⟵≪

Here's some advice if you plan on taking the Number 7 down Bathurst Street at 7:36 a.m. Do *not* sit downwind from the woman eating the industrial-grade tuna fish. And if The Groomer is on the bus, get ready to duck at the first sign of the nail clippers.

You really don't want any more details. And neither did I. But by my third morning in Toronto, I could have taught a class in Number 7 Studies. Which is what happens when you vacuum-pack the population of Giants Stadium into a space the size of a hot tub. I grasped a slimy pole next to the bus driver (nametag: Ian), where the air was only slightly less gloopy. I was just learning about Ian's path to driver-dom when he broke the unfortunate news.

"You'll have to move to the back now."

Ian was the closest thing that I had to a friend in Toronto.

O Leah, where art thou?

I glanced down at my cell phone but there was still no word from my sister. She was probably just boarding the bus in New York's Port Authority with her wedding gown wrapped in layers of tissue paper and nestled safely in the garment box. I had sixteen hours until I could meet the gown in person.

I took a deep breath and squeezed myself through the maze of human heat machines to the rear of the bus. Craning my neck, I caught sight of the ginger-haired woman reading in a seat next to the sealed window. Two boys clinging to an overhead pole ogled her from above.

Her red hair was swept back in a half-bun today. Tiny ringlets spilled onto her shoulders. She wore a silky Marc Jacobs blouse that I recognized from Macy's, a dark twill skirt that covered her knees, and pantyhose.

The elderly man sitting next to her struggled to his feet and pushed his way toward the exit. I squeezed past a child barking into a cell phone and plopped into the empty seat beside the woman.

Gingie-Locks's eyes were trained on the book resting in her lap. I glanced over her shoulder and noticed the word "love" sprinkled across the page. The title was written in a tiny font at the top of the open book. I leaned over and pretended to adjust the bow on my right shoe so I could make out the name of the book. *Hope and Inspiration for the Single Soul.*

I could use a little of that myself these days. I leaned back and peered past her, out the window. *How on earth was I going to survive this exile?*

The bouncing rhythm of "Sweet Caroline" hummed inside my handbag, offering a fleeting sense of the Red Sox. Unfortunately I wasn't at Fenway Park in the middle of the eighth inning — I was on the Number 7 bus holding a new phone. And since only three people had the number and my parents had called last night, there was only one person left.

My aunt. Mira Bernstein.

"Are you at school yet?" she said. "I noticed you left a little later than I suggested." Aunt Mira's prying voice might as well have been piped in over the bus's loudspeaker.

"I'm still on the bus," I said in a whisper.

"Fine. I'll call you later." By later, of course, she meant within the next twenty minutes. At this rate, I had to assume I was going to wake up one morning and find a GPS tracker clamped to my leg. This was my life as a Prisoner of Bernstein. It was painfully obvious that this year was not going to be a piece of cake. And speaking of cake, I don't mean to sound nasty but Aunt Mira's food wasn't exactly going to explode the ratings on RateMyMeatloaf.com, if you get what I'm saying.

If living with my mother's alpha sister wasn't bad enough, there was my sweet uncle Eli. Born and raised in Toronto, he had a tragic flaw. He was a Yankees fan. (Thank you Columbia Law School, class of '83.) I'm sorry, I adore you, New York, but I was born in *Massachusetts* for crying out loud. Couldn't he just root for something harmless like the Blue Jays?

I closed my eyes, but that only seemed to enhance the stink of body odour permeating the bus. It seemed so unfair that one un-showered person could hog all the clean air.

I dropped the phone back into my handbag. The only thing that was going to save me this year was my sister, Leah. Until November second she'd be all mine at Mira's, and then?

The wedding!

It didn't matter that I had been stuck in Hong Kong with Mom and Dad all summer while Leah was still in New York. Thanks to the internet, we swam the waters of bridal magazines, wedding gowns, and floral arrangements like pros — we were like the sockeye salmon of wedding planning. I hadn't heard from her since she'd gone down to New York on Thursday and was dying for details. As for Ben, her groom-to-be, there was still time to get used to him, I guess.

With nothing else to do I peered down at *Hope and Inspiration for the Single Soul*. Gingie-Locks was completely engrossed in her book. I strained my neck to get a better view.

She was reading a story about thirty-eight-year-old "Rachel Schwartz," who had given up hope of ever finding a mate after experiencing two broken engagements and a string of failed relationships. When it looked like things couldn't possibly get any worse, she suffered a terrible car accident and was rushed to the emergency room with a smashed-up foot.

Her encounter with the on-call podiatrist changed her life forever. They were instantly drawn to each other, started dating, and eventually got married in a fairy tale wedding. Not a bad story at all.

I was jarred out of Rachel Schwartz's honeymoon when Gingie-Locks turned in her seat. She took a sip from her travel coffee mug, looked at me with fern green eyes, and asked in an affable voice, "Am I reading too quickly for you?"

I gulped. "Um . . . no. It's perfect."

She smiled and nodded, then peered down at the book again.

I sighed. For the last two years in New York, I was free as the wind. And now? I couldn't even steal a glance without getting busted.

chapter 2

All dirty bricks and token windows, the Moriah Hebrew High School for Girls squatted sadly on a tract of exhausted shrubs. Winding through a bustle of girls I entered the building and managed to navigate my way to homeroom for English. It was my third day in eleventh grade at Moriah and I started class as I always did when I found myself at yet another new school: studying my new classmates. I peered around the room while Miss Weiss took attendance.

"Rebecca Abramson."

Never let a set of great cheekbones go to waste. Some side-bangs and you'd be a stunner.

"Dahlia Engel."

You seem nice enough, but I'm thinking that your soul might be part graphing calculator.

"Shira Wasser."

Now we're talking.

Shira's strawberry blond hair fell in a loose crimp over her shoulders, cascading past tiny pearl earrings. Her starched white Oxford shirt rested perfectly on her navy pleated skirt. Somehow, on Shira, our school uniform looked like it was a Ralph Lauren.

Shira flipped her hair and pulled her shoulders back. "Here," she said, her voice ringing across the room.

Every class has a Shira, and every school has a ruling one too, although there's no question that a Toronto Shira isn't going to be in the same league as a New York Shira. Shiras are the kind of girls that decide whether a teacher controls a class or not. Shiras possess the sort of look you'll probably have within the year. Shiras are the standard by which all other girls view themselves.

I was a Shira during my glorious reign at the Maimonides High School for Girls in New York City. I sighed at the memory of two years of endless girlfriends, sleepovers, shopping trips, and pizza — pizza that was actually edible. It all started when I bumped into Maya and Danielle in Herald Square at a Macy's sale at the start of ninth grade. They were identical twins with chocolate brown eyes and black hair that flowed down their backs; within one week I became known as the "third twin," and the three of us spent endless hours together. For the first time in my life I finally had a best friend who wasn't my sister. Which is one of the perks of living in a city for more than five minutes. (Sorry, Dad. I love you with all my heart. The constant moving — not so much.)

When I entered high school my life completely transformed — from dorkulous to, well, fabulous.

You see, way back when a dude called Giovanni da Verrazzano set foot in Manhattan, he encountered corn crops, beans, and forests. When *I* went to high school in the city, I discovered Stella, Ralph, and Calvin. It was crazy how it all came together. I finally chucked my membership card to the Order of the Invisible, and boy had I arrived!

But that was then and this was now. I couldn't believe that I was starting all over again — but at least my sister, Leah, would be in Toronto in mere hours.

While Miss Weiss continued taking attendance, the door opened and a freshie poked her head in the classroom.

"Mrs. Levine would like to speak to Raina Resnick."

The principal's office already? What could she want from me now? My eyes met Shira Wasser's. With her stare fixed on me she leaned over to the girl next to her and whispered. My cheeks burned as they both giggled.

I plodded down the hall with an uneasy feeling about Mrs. Levine. From our first meeting last June it was clear that I was less high school student, and more rehabilitation project. Her personal urban wetland, if you will.

I entered her office where she was ensconced behind her enormous fake-wood desk. Mrs. Levine sat ramrod straight, her falcon-like eyes trailing me as I lowered myself into the moulded plastic chair facing her.

A manila file folder with my name written in black marker lay on her desk next to a cluster of photos of her with her children and grandchildren. In one of them, Mrs. Levine was sitting on a park bench hugging her young grandson. There was something not quite right about the image — like someone had Photoshopped a smile onto her face.

"I trust that you're having a positive adjustment to Toronto," she said, her stare as animated as a frozen flounder. "I'm quite pleased that your sister will be living with your aunt until her wedding. I understand she's a very studious young lady."

Which was code for responsible, of course. With our matching black hair and turquoise eyes, Leah and I looked alike on the outside, but to be honest, she really *was* the good one. I mean, until she fell in love and disappeared into the Ben-o-verse last year, she was the one who had gotten me through my math and science classes. She was the one I could count on for friendship, no matter what city we were in. Which is pretty impressive for a sibling who's seven years older.

"And you're both living in such a lovely community," Mrs. Levine was saying.

You kidding me? What's *not* to love about Thornhill? It's the suburb that never sleeps!

She placed her clasped hands on the table and trained her eyes on me.

And trained and trained.

I shifted in my seat and waited. The ticking of the industrial clock thumped the heavy air in the room. A picture of a rabbi in a black coat hung on the wall behind her.

"I'm not going to lie, Raina," she finally said. "You *know* that I have concerns that our academic standards aren't necessarily the best . . . match for you."

Her eyes were like laser beams; it seemed dangerous to look at them directly.

"I do hope you're settling in at Moriah," she said. Talk about settling in, I stared at her hair. What was with women in their sixties sporting hairstyles so stiff they looked like they'd been sprayed with polyurethane?

"Raina?"

"Oh, sorry. I'm extremely settled."

Mrs. Levine shot me another one of her trademark x-ray gazes. I tightened my unbuttoned blazer around me, like I could gaze-proof myself.

"This is a critical opportunity that you have now," she said. She pinched her lips together, rose from her seat, rounded the table, and then settled on the edge of the desk. Her blouse was rammed inside a skirt with an elastic waistband that was exactly eye level. I would never want to alarm Mrs. Levine, but with all that polyester she was a walking fire hazard.

"Our program is *really* geared for the student who is *responsible* and *conscientious*," she said. "We have very strict rules here and since you signed a form saying that you've read and agreed to the student handbook, I'm not anticipating any problems. Attendance, punctuality, and especially cell phones. We do *not* tolerate cell phones at the school."

I craned my neck, mesmerized by the tiny bits of mist spraying down from her mouth. "But we do all want to maximize your opportunity for growth."

Like I was a financial portfolio. I stared longingly at the door to her office. Maybe Hong Kong wouldn't be so bad after all. As Mrs. Levine leaned forward I shrank back in my seat.

"I'm sure you're aware that I have concerns about the appropriateness of your placement here," she said, in case I'd missed it the first fifty times. "So to that end, you'll meet with me on a weekly basis, to check in on your progress. And we'd like to offer you the opportunity to meet with the school social worker, Mrs. Marmor, who is more than happy to help you in any way possible."

The "we" who were making this "offer" was a painfully vast network of adults who had conspired to arrange every aspect of my life since I was tossed out of Maimonides last June. We're talking principals, vice principals, parents, social workers, and psychologists. It was a dream team of teenage failure management.

"That's so sweet, Mrs. Levine, but I really don't think that's necessary."

"Thursdays at lunch," she said, without moving a muscle on her face. "Agreed?"

You could have choked from all the hostility in that office. I answered with a tiny nod.

When she finally released me, I stepped out the door of her office, just as Dahlia Engel dropped off a form in the reception area. She shot a glance at the office entrance and our eyes met for a moment. She quickly averted her gaze, like she'd been caught gawking at the bleeder next to the ambulance. I grimaced and shrunk back toward the office.

Pity. And from a geek like Dahlia Engel, no less. Does it get worse than that?

That night, after a nasty dinner of tuna patties and canned corn, I shuffled over to the dairy sink in the large kitchen island.

"Mira, *such* a delicious dinner," Bubby Bayla said, as she choked down a bite of her tuna patty. Aunt Mira's mother-in-law was a thick woman in her eighties with wispy silver curls, sensible frames, and a doughy face.

The heat wave was stifling so I splashed some cold water on my cheeks. Aunt Mira, wearing a silk blouse with a tied bow, plucked a tea towel from a cherry cabinet and handed it to me. I grabbed it and wiped my sweaty face.

Big mistake.

I was sure I heard a snort from Bubby Bayla. Mira pursed her lips and said in a Very. Controlled. Tone, "Raina."

Okay, *now* what did I do?

"That's for drying dishes," Aunt Mira said. "For *you* to dry dishes with."

"Don't they dry if you just leave them out?"

Bubby chuckled. Mira placed her fists on her hips and glared. I got it now. The plan was for me to become Mira's beast of burden.

Jeremy regarded me from over his cantaloupe with a bemused smile.

How do I begin to explain Jeremy?

Actually, maybe somebody could explain to me why an able-bodied thirty-year-old lawyer was practically squatting at Mira's house? I know that his dad was best friends with Uncle Eli back in law school, but really, didn't he have some bachelor pad that he could, you know, *live in*?

"What do you think of Sabathia's performance?" Uncle Eli said, turning to Jeremy. Did he have to bring up a Yankee so soon after dinner? It made me want to bring up mine.

"He just has an incredible arm," Jeremy said, knuckling the table for emphasis.

Bubby shook her head and muttered something inaudible before pulling herself up to her feet and shuffling out of the kitchen. Uncle Eli and Jeremy watched her hobble to the family room where she settled herself on the couch with a moan.

Jeremy turned back to Uncle Eli. "He's one of the most dependable pitchers in the league," he said, winking at me.

I spun away from him and attacked the ceramic dish. Jeremy, like Uncle Eli, was a shameless Yankees fan. Which probably would explain why he was having such a hard time finding a wife.

The ringing of my phone rescued me from the coven of heretics.

"Hi sweetie, are you okay?" It was my father calling from Hong Kong. "Mom's wondering how school is going."

Translation: *Has there been any trouble yet?*

I inched away from the kitchen into the family room where Bubby was now dozing on the leather couch. Something about his voice made me start to lose it.

"You're driving down to the bus station in a few hours to get Leah?" he said.

I'm counting the seconds. "Uncle Eli's taking me," I said as I balanced on the arm of the couch.

"I think there's something she's going to want to discuss with you," he said in a quiet voice.

Jeremy slapped on a Yankees cap and waved at me before sauntering out of the kitchen.

I croaked into the phone. "What do I do about Uncle Eli?"

"Oh Rainy, I'm sorry," he said. "Just agree to disagree."

I lowered my voice to a whisper. "Dad, it's one thing to have a conversation, but to *share a house* with a Yankees fan?"

chapter 3
If You Have an Older Sister

Uncle Eli pulled his black Volvo onto Edward Street. "Why don't I wait in the car and you can go into the terminal and find her," he said. "I'm sure you'll want to spend a few minutes alone together."

"Sure," I said as I sprang out of the passenger seat into the muggy September night. There was lightness in my gait — Leah was back! When I was younger we moved between so many cities, but the one constant was Leah. How many older sisters would let you tag along with their friends and cling to them in public? Or take you to museums, and share their secrets? If you have an older sister, you really do want one like Leah.

I kind of lost Leah after she met Ben last October, but everything changed over the summer. And after bonding again, we would have two glorious months to prepare for the wedding together.

I scooted between two parked Greyhound buses and sprinted into a hangar with buses lined up in a row, each one belching competing levels of exhaust. Scanning for the arrivals, I caught sight of a familiar head of crimped curls.

"Hey, Shira!" I called.

She swerved around and stared blankly.

"Hi. I'm Rain Resnick?" I said with my finger on my chest. "I'm at Moriah this year. We're in a bunch of classes together?"

"Right," she said with a slight nod. "Hi."

"I'm waiting for my sister to come in from New York," I said. "You?"

"My cousin's coming in from New York too," she said as she watched a bus glide into the bay. The front door burst open, and an elderly Asian man hobbled down the stairs, followed by a string of haggard passengers.

Leah finally descended the steps of the bus, the twelve-hour journey written on her face. Strands of hair from a makeshift ponytail straggled past mascara-smeared eyes. I flew at her and wrapped her in a hug.

"We're blocking people," she said in a quiet voice.

"Let me take your bag," I said as I grabbed her suitcase. "I'm so excited you're here! Where's the gown?"

"I don't have it," she said. She craned her neck in search of the exit.

I stopped. "What?" That was the whole purpose of the trip. "Where's Uncle Eli?"

I pointed to the waiting car. "Is everything okay?"

Leah charged out of the station without saying a word. Shira's arms were crossed as she watched us. My cheeks tingled as I scrambled after Leah.

Out on the street Uncle Eli waved at us.

"Hi, Uncle Eli, thanks so much for getting me," Leah said as she slid into the passenger seat. Eli popped the trunk open and dropped in her bag.

"Did she tell you?" he murmured to me.

An angry wind whooshed past us, slamming his door closed. "What's going on?" I said, as I gathered my hair.

He clapped the trunk shut and sighed.

"Uncle Eli, please," I said.

He turned to me, his face marked by uncle-type pain. "Rain, there's something you need to know."

I braced myself.

"Leah's engagement is off. Leah and Ben aren't getting married."

chapter 4
Queen of the Nobodies

Leah's heartbreak coated the Bernstein household in a thick layer of sadness. In good times her joy could radiate across a room and fill every nook and crevice with sunlight. But now she was a tiny flame that had been doused with a thousand buckets of pain. And I couldn't get any answers.

Rain, she doesn't want to talk about it.

Rain, just let her be. She's hurting.

She hadn't said a word to me since her return from New York. When we passed each other in the house, I may as well have been a ghost. She spent more time chatting with Bubby Bayla than me, her best friend. (Sorry, *former* best friend.) And considering that Leah's conversation with Bubby averaged less than twenty seconds, you can get an idea of where I stood with her.

On Sunday, I stepped into the kitchen on a mandarin orange mission and found Leah seated at the computer desk. She looked up briefly. Her side-swept bangs and straight hair contoured pale skin with ocean blue eyes that darkened when they saw me.

"Hey," I said as I opened the fridge.

She continued typing. I turned around and glanced at the computer screen.

Leah was on her all-time favourite site, MazelTovNation. She clicked on New York and scrolled through the listing of couples engaged in the last week. When she'd exhausted the New York announcements, she tapped on the Canada icon and began searching though the local engagement notices.

MazelTovNation was Leah's crack cocaine.

"Leah?" I ached to grab her and wrap her in a hug. I needed to cry with her and Leah needed to cry with me. "Can I do anything for you?"

Her hands froze on top of the keyboard.

"Please, Leah. Can we talk?"

She released a bitter laugh, exited the website, and rose from the chair. "It's too late, Rain. You got what you wanted anyway."

"What are you talking about?"

"Forget it." She strode past me, leaving a cold blast in her wake. I crumpled into a kitchen chair. Was Leah blaming *me* for the breakup? I'll admit I never totally trusted Ben. But maybe to me no one was good enough for Leah.

On paper Ben was perfect. He was cute and confident and a successful hedge-fund manager. When they weren't busy flying back and forth between Toronto and New York, they were either calling, texting, or Skypeing each other. He was a bit too smooth though; the way he constantly complimented my mother, or praised my father. Or himself. Leah was a beautiful ornament, but one that he didn't really take proper care of. He never seemed to be *there* for Leah. I knew that his boss was a nasty and controlling piece of work. Still, Ben cancelled plans and stood Leah up far too often.

And then there was the argument.

It was on the Sunday of the Fourth of July weekend, a week before I left for Hong Kong to spend the rest of the summer with Mom and Dad. Leah had planned a barbecue to introduce Ben to some of her friends at Aunt Naomi's house in Brooklyn. The yard was decorated with red, white, and blue streamers. The chicken and hot dogs were ready to grill and a huge bowl of punch sat on the aluminum table. The guests had all arrived.

But Ben never did.

He called later Sunday night to apologize for a last minute business trip out to San Diego and to curse his boss for being such a despot and threatening him with his job. Leah forgave him.

I did not.

The following weekend Leah finally offered me a release from my misery. "Okay, Rain," she said. "What's wrong? Let's talk."

"I'm still *furious*," I said.

She shook her head. "Why?"

"The barbecue."

She sighed. "Still? You know Ben's boss is a misery."

"He could have called first. What, there's no phone on the

way to the airport? He had to wait until later that night? And you know it's not the first time either. He cancels and doesn't show up *all* the time. I don't trust him."

And so I went on. Ben was self-centred. Ben was inconsiderate. Ben was shallow. Ben was manipulative.

Ben was a lot of things, but worst of all Ben was there.

And I mean literally *there*. Standing at the door, listening to my rant. Ben and I exchanged words but then I noticed Leah's pleading eyes.

"She's a *nightmare*," he muttered under his breath to Leah as I stormed upstairs.

If that argument opened a rift between them that cascaded into a breakup then frankly, Ben was an idiot. What did their relationship have to do with me? Even if my words highlighted their problems, they were *their* problems. Ben was supposed to be marrying Leah — not me.

Leah had no right whatsoever to blame me, but living with this tension in the Bernsteins' house was unbearable. There was no escape, nowhere to go, and no one to hang out with.

If I thought I'd get any relief at my new high school, I was sadly mistaken. It felt as if Mrs. Levine's hostility to me had somehow leaked down into the student body and I had developed a case of terminal cooties. Beyond the polite smiles from Dahlia and the impolite glares from Shira, I wandered the halls of Moriah alone. I was the Queen of Nobodies.

Nice to see you again, elementary school!

My loneliness sprouted an idea.

If I could contact the person who had introduced Leah

and Ben, then maybe we could figure out a way to patch up their relationship. I'm sure my mom had the phone number.

So on Thursday, with my cell phone in hand, I plopped onto the bed of my new bedroom. It was actually my cousin Asher's old bedroom, before he got married and moved to New Jersey, which would be the only explanation for the fact that I was lying on a navy plaid comforter in a room wallpapered with faded Toronto Maple Leafs posters that were curling at the corners.

Was there anything right about this year?

I dialled my mother to get the story, because I still couldn't believe how Leah was blaming me. "Mom, what happened between Leah and Ben?"

"Sweetie, it's private. I know you're frustrated."

"But Mom —"

"How's school going?" she said in a bright voice.

"Okay, I guess," I said. "Mom, I can't remember who made Leah's match."

She laughed. "Rivky Marmor. She's the social worker at your new school."

I groaned. I had completely forgotten that Mom knew her through social work circles. Mrs. Marmor was the reason why Leah had met a Toronto boy.

I said goodbye to my mom so I could formulate my plan. This was not going to be fun. But at least now I could take some action.

At lunchtime the next day I managed to secure an impromptu appointment with Mrs. Marmor. Unlike Mrs. Levine's office, this was a cluttered girly space with self-esteem slogans plastered across every imaginable surface. It was blanketed with mugs, embroidered pillows, posters, and books that screamed instructions like "Confidence is rooted in conquering challenges!" or "Forget your fears and find your choices!" My favourite was the totally inane "Allow yourself to believe in yourself!" Even the mezuzah looked like it was fashioned from unchewed bubble gum.

Note to self: Take a Gravol if I ever come back.

Mrs. Marmor entered her office and slid into the chair next to me, unobstructed by the hostility of a desk. Her straight black hair fell past her shoulders onto a tailored charcoal blazer that perfectly matched her grey pencil skirt. She smiled and stared at me intensely, practically assaulting me with empathy.

"Raina! I'm so happy you *finally* came to see me. How *are* you? Are you *finding* the girls friendly here? Are you *making* friends?"

Let's see. Answers: Not Good. Girls Not Friendly. No Friends.

I shrugged.

"You've been through a lot. Moving to yet another city." She paused for effect. "Leaving your friends behind." Wrapped in a voice so velvety smooth, that compassion of hers could bore a hole through galvanized steel.

"Why don't you share with me how you're integrating into Moriah? Do you need help processing the incident at Maimonides with Mr. Sacks —"

"It's all processed now," I said. I grew up with the lingo and had pretty much developed psychotherapy-resistant antibodies. Still, you had to feel some sympathy, watching Mrs.

Marmor struggling so hard to stir up an emotional response in me.

"I'm very motivated to succeed," I said. "And I hope to work on my self-esteem issues with the goal of making emotionally intelligent choices." Honestly, I could spew this stuff in my sleep.

Mrs. Marmor still wasn't saying anything. The silence was unbearable and I was starting to feel crazed by this slow-motion conversation. I dropped my eyes and noticed her feet. Can someone explain to me why middle-aged women wear Mary Janes?

"Mrs. Marmor, those shoes are so cute," I said. "Are they from Walmart?"

"No, actually. But thank you anyway."

I waited.

"So how can I help you?" she finally said.

"It's about my sister Leah, and Ben," I said.

That's when she started nodding. And nodding and nodding. She looked like a bobble-head dog.

She finally snapped out of the trance. "You know what? I'm *so* happy you came." She leaned over and squeezed my wrist. "Everyone will be thrilled. Guilt can be extremely painful, debilitating even. But in the end it's a very destructive emotion."

I blinked.

"But *regret* on the other hand? That's something we can work with."

I wrinkled my nose. "I'm not sure if I was clear," I said. "I . . . was talking about Leah and Ben."

"Exactly," she said.

"I don't get it."

The friendly smile vanished from her face and she stared

at me with a Mrs. Levine–grade gaze. Mrs. Marmor's Temple of Self-Esteem was feeling a little claustrophobic now. She cocked her head to one side, clasped her hands in her lap, and continued the stare. "Either way, I'm so glad you came today, Rain. We're going to chart a new course together."

I wasn't so sure about that. Even if I did decide to do any charting, it sure wasn't going to be with Mrs. Marmor. So Ben and I might not have gotten along, but I'm sorry, it was ridiculous to blame me for the breakup. Maybe Mrs. Marmor was just upset because it was *her* match. "Are you saying that I broke up their relationship?"

She cocked her head to the side. "Nobody spoke to you about what happened?"

I sliced the air with my hand. "Nothing. Silence."

She started nodding again, but I had no patience to wait for another bobbing period to pass.

"Don't you think it's a stretch to blame me for their split?" I mean, was I supposed to be in love with Ben too?

Any remnant of empathy seemed to drain from her face, leaving disbelief in its place. I shrank back in my seat.

"I can't divulge personal details," she said. "But I certainly think some personal responsibility on your part would be in order here."

"I didn't do anything," I said.

"I'm sorry. I've said too much already. I suggest you speak to your mother." She shook her head as she rose to her feet and strode to the door. The meeting was over.

She walked me past the reception area to the threshold of the hallway where throngs of girls sailed by. Apparently she was under the impression that high school students enjoy being viewed publicly with the staff shrink.

chapter 5

Running Out of Rosenbergs

You know things are bad when even the school shrink is mad at you. September had turned out to be one big fail. Rosh Hashanah was a quiet, lonely affair without friends or laughter or most of all — Leah. My annoyance at her blaming me was definitely outweighed by her absence from my life.

At this point I was down to my bus buddy, Gingie-Locks. Bonded by nothing more than tales of wedded bliss, she was all I had, even though we had barely spoken a word to each other.

It took us around a week to finish reading *Hope and Inspiration for the Single Soul*. The second week we covered *Jewish Paths to Love and Marriage*. I thought I'd read every possible variation of dating stories with happy endings, but then she brought in *From Dating Disaster to Happily Ever After: A Jewish Perspective.* Who knew that this number of misery-to-marriage stories was even mathematically possible? Every day the trip to school became a harrowing journey that lurched from the depths of despair to the apex of romantic love. I was emotionally exhausted by the time I got off the bus.

It didn't replace Leah and her cancelled wedding, but this stranger was all I had. By the beginning of October we finished the rather far-fetched *Finally Finding Love: 100 True Tales.* She shut it and shook her head with a chuckle, tendrils of hair bouncing on her shoulders.

"No way, huh?" I said.

"I'd say ten are true. And the other ninety?" She shrugged and shoved the book back in her handbag. *"Tales."*

"Like who actually falls in love with the man who's about to remove your gallbladder."

"And what's a municipal hygiene operative, anyways?" she said, wrinkling her nose. We both shuddered. She zipped her bag and turned to me with a broad smile. "So what do you do?"

A charge of excitement coursed through me. It looked like our relationship was going to go to the next level. The one where people actually speak.

"Nothing." I shook my head and threw my palms up in the air. "I'm a student."

"Ah, got it." She pointed at my navy skirt. "That's the Moriah uniform. But I don't remember seeing you on this route last year." The bus came to a stop and a small crowd of people exited. More air for the rest of us.

"I'm from New York," I said. "Actually, I moved there from Boston when I was fourteen. My dad was transferred to Hong

Kong for his job two years ago and I even spent the summer there but that was as much as I could take, so here I am."

"Wouldn't Hong Kong be kind of interesting?"

"Nope." I shook my head.

She arched her eyebrow.

I leaned back against the plastic seat. "I was born in Boston but we moved to Baltimore when I was four." I held up my hand and started counting my fingers. "Then we moved to Providence, then New Haven, and then back to Boston for seventh grade. So when my parents left, I moved in with my mother's sister, Naomi. She lives in Brooklyn."

"Oy," she said.

"My dad works for a bank. We call it the City-after-city bank. We had to keep moving for his job," I said. "The only friend I had until high school was my sister." An invisible fist socked my stomach when I thought of her. I swallowed hard; the words had just tumbled out of me. I finally had someone to whine to and it felt awesome.

"But why aren't you still in New York?" She clasped her hands in her lap, waiting for a good story.

My stomach tightened. "My parents wanted me to be in a less . . . distracting environment."

I wasn't exactly keen to share the details with her but the two years since my parents had relocated to Hong Kong were like a big bath of awesome. Aunt Naomi is what you would call the more . . . *defenseless* of my mom's two sisters. After being "counselled" out of Maimonides, I was deported to Aunt Mira's house with strict instructions to academically excel or else say hello to Hong Kong Homeschool (otherwise known as my parents' living room) with a high school diploma through correspondence classes. I mean, it's a nice place and all, but not exactly my natural habitat. How many times can you visit the Pacific Mall? Without your besties?

My mom had become fond of pointing out that if I blew this year at her second sister's place, I'd officially run out of Rosenbergs. Mira, Mom, and Naomi were a formidable team of sisters, but this was all that was left.

"Where did you go to school in New York?" Gingie asked.

"Maimonides Girls," I mumbled, shifting in my seat. I guess the School Question was inevitable, but I *really* would have preferred to leave the embarrassing details of my expulsion behind.

"No way!" Her eyes widened in recognition. "My friend Aviva went there for her senior year!"

I felt my face turn crimson. Why do bad coincidences happen to good people?

You know what the problem is? When you're trying to move on with your life, Jewish Geography is a blood sport. Imagine a game show where you have seconds to figure out who you know in common.

The street outside was thick with traffic and the bus slowed to a crawl; the school suddenly seemed hours away. I needed to change the subject fast. "That's interesting," I said, and forced a smile. "My name's Rain, by the way. What's yours?"

"Tamara. Here, I'll give you my card." She rifled through her handbag, a Fendi style knockoff that somehow worked on her. She plucked out a business card and handed it to me. *Tamara Greenberg. Financial Consultant.*

"So you're a math person?" I said. "But you seem so nice!"

She laughed. "Not your favourite subject?"

I slowly shook my head, a motion powered by misery. This whole *year* was misery, and math was not exactly my priority.

She crinkled her eyes in a sympathetic smile. "What are you working on? Maybe I can help."

"Some sort of equations? I'm pathetic."

"Okay, let's see it," she said. I gave her a look. "Come on," she said, tapping my knapsack. "I insist."

I reluctantly pulled out the textbook and dropped it on her lap. For the rest of the twenty-minute ride and every day for the next week Tamara tutored me in math and even wrote out test questions to take home with me. And she was good.

With Tamara's help I actually made some progress. By the time we got to the end of the chapter, I actually knew what she was talking about. Sort of.

On Friday I tackled the math test like a linebacker. I was determined to pass to prove to Tamara that I was worthy of her attention. Miraculously I did, and when I saw Tamara the following Monday, nose buried in a book, I flopped into the seat next to her. I waved my paper with the big "B+" on it in front of her face before smothering her in a hug.

"Thank you, thank you, thank you," I said. You really do feel close to a person when you share that many polynomials.

"I'm so proud of you, Rain." She held my embrace. "You worked hard for it."

Tamara was pretty awesome. I guess if you're completely alone in Toronto with only one friend, it might as well be someone older who thinks equations are interesting. Especially since I'd cooled off on Ian the bus driver.

"I'm here for you," she said, releasing me. "Really, any time."

We leaned back and smiled at each other.

"What are we reading today?" I said, pointing to the book on her lap.

She raised the book to show me the cover with a self-conscious laugh. *Turning Lonesome into Twosome: Jewish Lessons in Love and Commitment.*

I fixed my gaze on her. "Not that they aren't fun, but what's with all the singles books?"

She smiled sadly. "I'm single — I'm twenty-eight."

"You're kidding," I blurted out, my mouth hanging open in shock.

And since you're probably wondering why that's a big deal, let me put it this way. You have to think dog years when you you're single in a traditional Jewish community. So twenty-eight was the equivalent of . . . a lot older. Even Leah, at twenty-three, was not going to be happy about being unmarried.

"It's not what I wanted," Tamara said, her voice betraying a tiny wobble. She leaned back in her seat and gazed out the cloudy window. "I've just had . . . a really hard time getting dates. No matchmakers have really taken me under their wing. Even when I do go out, for some reason they never seem to progress past three or four dates."

I couldn't hide my surprise. Tamara may not have been a supermodel or anything, but she was certainly nice to look at. Her orange ringlets outlined a sweet-natured face with a soft complexion. And she was smart, funny, and kind.

"But you're *awesome.*"

She shook her head. "You wouldn't believe how hard it is to find someone."

Maybe Leah had gotten more dates because New York had a bigger community than Toronto. In fact, it reminded me a lot of the conversation over at the Bernsteins whenever Jeremy was around. "Sounds like Jeremy," I muttered.

"Who?"

"Oh just this guy who practically lives at my aunt's place. They're all lawyers. So he's become like a permanent house guest since he moved from Albany and passed the bar here."

"And he's single?" Tamara twirled a lock of hair around her index finger.

"Yes. He's very single. It's like he doesn't have a life. He's *always there*," I said, throwing my hands up.

"Tell me more," she said in a soft voice.

The bus ground to a halt and the engine shut down with a belch, leaving a sound vacuum.

I lowered my voice. "It's no joke. I have no *space* in that house. He's always watching me get chewed out by my aunt. And when he talks it's either blah blah law, or blah blah food package deliveries, or blah blah animal shelter."

Tamara's eyes widened. "Food package deliveries? Animal shelter?"

"Yeah, he does deliveries every Thursday night. He also does volunteer legal work for this shelter that I've already heard about a thousand times. Anyways, of *course* he doesn't have a girlfriend," I said. "He's obviously only comfortable with the elderly and with dogs. In fact I'll bet he only likes elderly dogs."

Tamara was listening raptly, drinking in every word.

"Anyways, you know what's the worst thing?" I was unstoppable now. "He's a Yankees fan."

Tamara chuckled. Like that was a *joke*. "So maybe he just needs someone who doesn't care about baseball," she said with wide eyes.

The engine of the bus finally revved up.

Tamara cleared her throat and tucked another lock behind her ear. "He sounds interesting."

"Please." I snorted. "You could do *so* much better than Jeremy Koenig."

She shook her head. "I don't know about that."

"Have you tried Rivky Marmor? She fixed up my —"

I bit my lip. It wasn't like Tamara could call her up and use me as a reference.

"I've actually been in contact with and even met with her, but she's never fixed me up."

I slumped back into my seat, spent from my rant. "Don't give up so easily. I really wish I could help you find an amazing guy. You're so wonderful and you've been amazing to me."

She smiled. "Sometimes we're just put in unexpected situations where we can help people. I'm always happy to help you."

I looked at my only friend in Toronto. "You are so awesome. I actually *passed a math test* because of you. I really, *really* would do anything to help you too."

She closed her eyes and squeezed her lips together. "Thank you," she said in a whisper, like she was about to cry.

"Come again?"

"It really has been impossible for me to find anyone to date," she said, her cheeks reddening. "It sounds like Jeremy and I have a lot in common. I mean I really like that he does all that volunteering. You are so sweet." She grabbed my hand in hers. "I really, really appreciate this." Even her complexion was the colour of gratitude.

My mouth fell open.

Did I just agree to a *set-up*?

"I've been searching for a really kind man," she murmured. "This means so much to me."

How the heck did this just happen?

She squeezed my hand and peered at me, her eyes two big pools of heartfelt gratitude.

Oh. No.

Now before you think that fixing up a stranger on the bus is completely bizarre, there are more things you need to understand about my Jewish community.

Rules for Dating in My World

#1. You're married with a family by your mid-twenties. That's because if you know anyone single . . . you fix them up.

#2. Even if you met someone five minutes ago, they're technically no longer a stranger. You fix them up.

#3. It doesn't matter how old or young you are yourself. You fix them up.

See the pattern here?

I knew that setting her up would be the right thing to do but I wasn't exactly known for doing the right thing since my expulsion from Maimonides. To be honest, I just didn't think I had the stomach for matchmaking. My mom's made her fair share of matches over the years. In fact, she probably found the only two Jews in Hong Kong and had them on a date right now. The problem is, in my community the matchmaker's job isn't done until the engagement — or the breakup. She's there to mediate and advise.

What if things went bad between Jeremy and Tamara? Did I really want to risk losing the one and only friend I had in Toronto now that Leah had cut me out?

Nuh-uh.

I really needed to learn how to think before I blurted. I glanced out the window, willing the bus to arrive at my stop already. How had I got myself into this?

The only bright side was that it might just be a fantastic opportunity to offload Jeremy. What if Leah considered dating him when she was ready to go out again? Yankees fan brother-in-law?

No way.

It didn't seem to bother Tamara. Everyone's always looking for perfection, but Tamara was obviously decent enough to overlook that kind of flaw in another human being.

I twisted my hands together on my lap and sighed. Maybe I needed to do something good and bring two people together. And if it worked, I could give Tamara some happiness.

I sighed. "I'll talk to Jeremy next time I see him."

She beamed at me.

"I don't really know how to ask him," I said.

"You'll be perfect. How about if you and I meet at the library," she said. "They have a little coffee shop." She was dangling friendship in front of me like red meat. It was October and I was getting desperate.

"Okay," I said.

Tamara threw her arm around my shoulder and gave me a light squeeze. Me making a match? Pretty crazy, huh? I'm sixteen years old and have never been on a date. So what do I know about fixing anybody up. But you want to know what's nuttier?

I did it.

chapter 6

Friday night was the beginning of Shabbos. From sundown to darkness on Saturday, time stands still, and you're unwired for twenty-five hours of calm. It gave me the chance to approach Jeremy when he came over for dinner. He stood at a stringy six feet, with chestnut eyes and a lock of black hair falling over his forehead. I hadn't really paid much attention to his appearance before but now that I really looked at him, he didn't score too badly on the looks scale.

When he and Uncle Eli came home from *shul* he wandered into the family room while my aunt and Leah puttered around the kitchen putting last-minute touches on the salads. Leah had made a fine chicken soup and the smell wafted through the air, beckoning me to the kitchen, but I held my ground. Jeremy smiled at me and sank into the leather recliner. I positioned myself across from him on the matching couch, watching him leaf through a copy of *Jewish Family Life* magazine. He glanced up at me with a quizzical smile.

I swallowed hard and glanced at the hallway. Mira, Eli, and Leah were drifting to the dining room table, where Bubby was already sitting and waiting, spoon in hand.

I cleared my throat. "Um . . . how was *shul*?"

Jeremy lowered the magazine to his lap. "Well, I guess it was —"

There didn't seem to be an elegant way of doing this. "I think . . . I might have met someone for you," I blurted out. I could feel my face flush. The words fell out like they were trespassing private property. "A single woman who is just awesome."

His eyebrows shot up. "You mean your sister?" It felt like my *eyeballs* were turning red now.

I cleared my throat. "No." I shook my head. "There's no way that she's dating yet."

"Yeah, I was wondering about that," he said, dropping the magazine back in the rattan basket.

"This one is really special."

Jeremy nodded slowly. "I'm listening."

"She's a financial consultant," I said. "She's really pretty. And sweet."

"Age?" He was actually considering this.

"Twenty-eight."

"She lives in the city?" he asked.

"Yes."

"From Toronto?"

"No, Vancouver."

Jeremy grasped his chin and squinted in concentration for a moment. Leah walked past the doorway with a dish towel in her hands, her eyes flicking at me. I squirmed in my seat until Leah returned to Aunt Mira. Her breakup with Ben was fresh enough that she didn't need to hear about any set-ups going on around her.

"And you personally recommend her?" Jeremy said.

"I do," I said, feeling tension draining from my body. "I really, really like her."

"Well, you're Mira and Eli's niece and they mean a lot to me." He leaned back in the recliner chair and gazed at the ceiling. "Give me a day to think about it."

I wanted to pump my fists. "You're open?"

"I'm open," he said with a nod. "And thank you." He sauntered to the dining room, leaving me alone in the den where I leapt to my feet and danced a private jig. Jeremy and Tamara — I might have pulled this off!

Who knew that matching up two people could be so oddly thrilling?

After dinner the following Thursday, the smell of Mira's meatloaf hung in the air like mustard gas. I couldn't wait to get to the library. In the six days since my conversation with Jeremy, *they'd seen each other four times*!

My bus rides with Tamara just weren't long enough to give me what I craved more than anything.

Details.

I needed details.

"Aunt Mira, can I use your car to go the library?"

"Why not," Mira said as she wiped down the granite counter. "Just be back by nine."

Uncle Eli wandered over to the dishwasher and tucked his plate inside. "Did you hear that Jeremy is dating someone?" he said.

I swerved around to him. "I know! It's so —"

"What?" Mira yelled.

"It's wonderful, isn't it?" Eli said. "Maybe that's why we haven't been seeing him all week."

Leah's mouth hung open, and a tiny croak came out. She spun around and fled from the kitchen.

We stood in silence until Eli spread his hands. "What did I say?"

Was Leah still that raw from the break-up?

Mira slammed the dishwasher door shut. "He was supposed to go out with *Leah.*"

He was?

Eli palmed the side of his head. "Me and my big mouth."

This was obviously the work of the Jewish grapevine. If I had to describe that grapevine I'd say it was what the internet was dreaming of becoming one day. "Fast" doesn't even begin to describe it. From the kitchen table, where I thought I detected a slight chortle, Bubby was watching events unfold.

"Why would Jeremy do that?" Mira said as she flung the dishrag into the sink. "He knew I wanted to fix him up with Leah. She was interested too."

She was?

So is *that* why the Bernsteins kept inviting him over? How was I supposed to know that Leah was ready to date again? If fixing Jeremy up with Leah had been the Bernstein plan, then I was in some deep trouble here.

I dropped into Aunt Mira's Camry with a blend of conflicting emotions brewing in my head. I should have been feeling charged that I finally had my first social outing. But my excitement for Tamara to give me the 411 on her and Jeremy was drowned out by the terror of being exposed as the one who introduced Jeremy and Tamara. I didn't need to give Leah more reason to be mad at me.

I drove to the library, or at least I tried to. Whoever designed this neighbourhood apparently didn't want anyone to leave. I motored through a confusing maze of streets — each one named after somebody's grandmother — just rows and rows of identical houses, each one hiding behind a big boxy garage. The trees were bare now, having shaken off the last of their dazzling autumn leaves into crunchy mounds along the roads. I finally arrived at the library, entered the building, and sucked in the scent of Java coffee beans and hazelnut. I dug my hand in my purse, dismayed to realize I had forgotten my cell. I padded over to a pay phone on the wall and dialled Jeremy. He picked up right after the first ring, which definitely bumped up his score on the dork-o-meter.

"Hi, Jeremy," I said. "It's me, Rain."

There was a moment of silence, then he exhaled loudly on the other end.

"Rain, I *like* Tamara. I mean I *really, really* like her. I don't even know how to thank you."

Yes!

"Jeremy, I have a problem," I blurted out. "I didn't realize that Leah actually wanted to go out with you. And she's already mad at me."

"Hmmm," he said. "No worries. We don't have to tell anyone that you introduced us. It'll be our secret."

I exhaled a sigh of relief. "Aunt Mira can't find out either. I think she was almost as upset as Leah."

"That's sort of news to me. But either way it's not a problem. By the way, is this your cell phone number? How do I reach you if I need to or should I call you at the Bernsteins? You *are* the matchmaker, after all," he said with a laugh.

Of course he might need to reach me. I had made one initial phone call to him with Tamara's number but now that I was playing the role of traditional matchmaker, I had to be available to mediate problems and situations. "I don't think you should call me on my cell phone," I said. "Aunt Mira shares a cell with Uncle Eli so she borrows mine sometimes. I wouldn't want her to recognize your number."

Which was a more dignified way of saying that I lived under the grip of Mira's electronic surveillance.

"Well, I love your aunt and uncle too and don't want them to be upset with me either," he said. "What about email?"

My mind started racing. The IMAX-sized computer monitor in the kitchen was not exactly conducive to secret matchmaking.

"She can access my email on my phone!" I thought out loud. If I put a password on my cell phone, Aunt Mira would become immediately suspicious.

"Set up an anonymous email account." Jeremy laughed. "Call it Matchmaven."

I considered that. "I guess that could work."

I jumped when a soft tap on my shoulder interrupted the call. I spun around to find Tamara smiling next to me.

"It's Jeremy," I whispered, pointing at the phone.

"Oh," she said, blushing. "Can I say hello?"

I handed Tamara the phone and studied her. She leaned into the receiver, her face, shoulders, and arms charged by an invisible current that ran out of that phone. Even though she was six inches away from me, she might as well have been in another country. A country with a citizenry of two, I might add, and since I wasn't one of them, I decided to give her some space.

My heart sailed — Tamara and Jeremy were falling in love! Even though I wasn't a member of their private universe, I was practically intoxicated from the effects of secondhand bliss. I skipped over the worn carpet to a display shelf and glanced at the books. I picked up a vegetarian cookbook and absently flipped through the pages.

Five eggplant casseroles later, Tamara was still deep in animated conversation. It looked like she couldn't be wrenched from that phone. Joy warmed me like a sunny Sunday at Fenway Park. I immediately found myself wandering over to the non-fiction section to search for my favourite number in the whole world.

796.35764.

It's true.

To me the number 796.35764 smells like freshly grilled hot dogs, cheesy nachos, and popcorn. It's the sound of David Ortiz cracking bat against ball, and the entire population of Fenway Park thundering to its feet and roaring with excitement. It's a humid summer breeze on the bleachers, wrapping me like a soft worn sweater.

796.35764 is Dewey for Red Sox, and in any library of any city we've ever lived in, that number always led me directly to the books about my beloved ball team.

I leafed through a pictorial volume about the American League Eastern Division until I finished the Red Sox chapter.

Tamara was still on the phone so I wandered over to the computer terminals where, taking Jeremy's suggestion, I set up my new email account and sent her my first email.

To: Tamara Green

From: Matchmaven <matchmaven@gmail.com>

I can see you from this computer and I can tell that you're having another awesome conversation with Jeremy. It looks like it's going really well. ☺ Kind of cool! Just one thing: I don't want my aunt or sister to know that I set you two up, so let's use this anonymous account.

xoxo,

Rain

I finally approached Tamara as she whispered a goodbye into the phone. She and Jeremy were so happening that I could have ordered up the stuffed chicken squab with roasted baby carrots for the wedding meal right then and there.

Tamara shrugged. "I'm so sorry —"

"Are you kidding?" I said. *"I just made a match!"*

"An amazing one," she said, her face stretched in a grin. "I just feel bad that I kept you waiting."

"Not at all," I said.

"Well, let's grab a coffee — my treat," she said.

Matchmaven. I really liked it. Maybe Jeremy wasn't so bad after all. Which just goes to show: you can never really judge a man by his ball club.

chapter 7
Hanging with the Old Guy

After a sleepless night, plotting different strategies for getting back into Leah's good graces, I traipsed into the kitchen where Aunt Mira, Leah, and Bubby Bayla were chatting.

"I'm so sorry, Aunt Mira," Leah said as she snatched her phone from her purse. "Let me see if I can switch my shift at the hospice tonight."

"Absolutely not, honey," Mira said, pushing down Leah's phone. "We'll figure something out."

"What about her?" Bubby Bayla grunted, pointing at me.

"What about me?" I said with a yawn as I opened the fridge.

"I *really* don't think that's going to work," Leah muttered.

"I don't see why not," Mira said. "That would solve the

problem. You could take the dinner out of the fridge and just drive it over."

I pulled out the Greek salad I was packing for my lunch. "Can I do it when I get home from school? I don't mind." Not that I wouldn't have minded crashing after school, after worrying about Leah all night.

"Aunt Mira, I'd be happy to do it," Leah said.

"I think I can do something as basic as delivering a meal," I said as I shoved my salad into my knapsack.

Of course I wouldn't mind delivering a meal for Mira. But since Leah obviously had zero faith in me, this little display of responsibility might convince her to like me a bit more. Or, more accurately, dislike me a bit less.

"I'm sure it won't be a problem for Raina." Mira glanced at her watch and grabbed her briefcase. "We have to leave now. I'll just leave instructions for when you get home. It'll be a huge help."

I plucked a green apple from the counter and followed Mira out the front door as Leah shook her head.

Something had to change because I hated being hated.

I looked forward to taking over that meal all day so that I could earn some Leah-points. A direct apology wasn't going to work, even though I didn't really think I owed her one. I still would have done it, though, if it would have put an end to the Deep Freeze. Reconciliation between Leah and Ben was out of the question, so I was down to delivering dinner. Like a brisket was going to salvage my relationship with my sister. But I still wasn't about to give up hope.

By the time I got to Ancient History class I'd been fretting about Leah for something like thirteen straight hours. I stumbled to my seat yawning, barely noticing when Dahlia got up to deliver a presentation on the Mesopotamian road to civilization. I don't really remember what happened before I lay my head on the desk.

A loud boom rang in my ears like a gunshot. I bolted upright in shock and gaped at the heavy textbook that Miss Gardner had slammed on my desk.

She loomed over me with her arms crossed. "Sorry to disturb you."

I looked up at her, still groggy. "Don't worry about it." Shira and Natalie were laughing uproariously, clutching each other's hands. Dahlia stood at the front of the class glowering at me.

"Do you think you can give Dahlia your attention now, Miss Resnick?"

I nodded and tried to ignore the tittering two rows over.

"I'm sorry, Miss Gardner. I've just been working really hard," I said, which was not a lie. Worrying was a lot of work, after all.

When I got home I found the note on the island countertop in the kitchen.

Hi Raina,
I need you to deliver a shiva meal to 141 Gladiola Drive
when you get home from school. There are three foil
pans in the fridge that you can take over in Uncle Eli's
car. Call me at work when you get home. Thank you for
helping out!
Love,
Aunt Mira

Oh. My. God.

A shiva house? I thought it was just an ordinary dinner! Please, no. I mean, does it get more awkward than visiting a person who's mourning for a lost family member for seven days? Someone I never even met?

I called up Mira.

"You've got the address," she said. "And you saw the pans?"

"Right."

"You'll be careful?" she said. "Take the food into the kitchen, maybe. Help out a bit."

I gulped. "Of course."

"And you know the shiva rules, right?" she said. "Don't ring the bell. Just take the food in the house. Let the mourner talk to you first."

"Of course."

Not.

I mean, sure I've *heard* of the rules, but let's face it — going to a shiva house is something your grandparents do. Or your parents. I found three foil pans in the fridge, stacked them in a pile, and carefully carried them out to the black passenger seat of Uncle Eli's Volvo. I pulled out of the driveway, the scent of cold lasagna combining with leather interior, through the chilly November night.

As I drove down Bathurst Street I glanced at the passenger seat and grimaced. I had forgotten Mira's note with the name and address on it. Luckily, I was good with directions, and I remembered the address anyway.

I arrived at the aging bungalow a few minutes later, where a rusting Crown Victoria sat in the driveway. Balancing the pans, I approached the front door. It opened easily and I stepped inside the front hall.

The house was so dim that I could barely make my way inside. I didn't realize that shiva houses were supposed to be so dark. As I approached the kitchen I peered into the living room on the right. Floor to ceiling bookcases plastered the walls. Stacks of books covered the coffee table and crowded the computer on the corner desk. What little air existed in that tiny house was permeated by the smell of book.

I found an elderly gentleman in his seventies in the musty kitchen. He sat alone at a table covered with oilcloth, sipping a cup of tea. He had a full head of white hair and watery brown eyes that shimmered behind gold spectacles.

Those big eyes blinked at me like I'd appeared out of thin air. "Can I help you, dear?"

"Oh . . . hi," I stammered. "I have . . . ah . . . dinner for you."

"You do." He blinked some more as he placed his teacup in the saucer. "And who are you?"

"Raina Resnick." I looked around to see if there was anybody else around who could rescue me.

"To what do I owe this honour?" he said.

"My aunt . . . Mira Bernstein . . . she sent this to you," I said, flustered. "Should I unpack everything? Sorry, I'm not really used to this."

"Neither am I, dear," he said with a sigh. His head dropped and he gazed at the floor.

I stood, unsure of what to do next.

"Why don't you have a seat?" he finally said.

I dropped into a vinyl chair with a lightning bolt of stuffing bursting out the back. Now what? We sat in silence for twenty-three hours.

Well, that's what those five minutes felt like, anyway. My

eyes wandered to an old coloured photograph on the fridge of a woman in a boxy suit with big hair and big glasses.

"Um, who have you lost?" I blurted out. "Your . . . wife?" *Bad, bad, bad.* Don't ask the mourners questions. Could I leave already?

He squeezed his eyes shut. In a panic I tried to think of something comforting.

"She must have been a . . . wonderful woman," I said.

His head tilted to the side and his gaze clouded. "She really was a remarkable woman," he said, his voice breaking. "When you lose someone that you love so dearly, it's a reminder of how much of a blessing it is to share such kinship."

"I'm so sorry." There was more silence. Was I supposed to ask him things? He obviously wanted me there, because he had invited me in. "Did she, um, also like to read a lot of books?"

"Yes. Our lives were filled with them." He stared off into the distance. My finger tapped the cold metal leg of the chair.

He finally came back to life. "Would you like to see more pictures of her?" he said, rising from his seat.

"Sure," I said, charging out of my chair so quickly I almost knocked him over.

At full height he was a lean man with a waistband that seemed to hover somewhere in the upper atmosphere. He led me to the dining room where a lace runner covering the mahogany credenza was crowded with photos of his children and grandchildren. I squinted at a portrait of three couples, probably taken at a wedding. This was clearly a man with fantastic vision because anyone who could possibly see anything in this darkness would have to be in the possession of super powers.

"Do your kids live in Toronto?" I said.

"No: I have two in Lakewood, New Jersey, and one in Israel."

I wandered over to a bookshelf and looked at the titles: *The Complete Annotated Yeats* and *Understanding Walt Whitman*. Another bookcase was lined with volumes about Shakespeare, and another one had titles like *Studies in Applied Biochemistry*.

Speaking of chemistry, I really needed to check my emails. To be honest, I was addicted to Tamara and Jeremy's relationship.

"I think I need to get going," I said.

He looked so heartbroken that I felt compelled to offer an excuse. "It's just that I have to check my email."

He pointed to the computer desk in the corner of the living room. "You're more than welcome to use my computer here," he said. "I'll just go and have some of that delicious-looking dinner while you do that."

It wasn't a bad offer at all. I liked the privacy here as well as the points I could score with Aunt Mira and Leah for hanging with the old guy. This house reeked of sadness. Kind of like my social life right now. What was even more depressing was the fact that he actually found Mira's food appetizing. I mean what was he living on? Fish entrails and boiled chicken?

Wait a minute. Isn't that what I was getting at Mira's house? There — more reasons to be bitter. In any case, I decided to take him up on his offer to use his computer. "Thanks," I said. "I'd love to."

"Wonderful. Any time you'd like to visit you're more than welcome."

"Oh, sure. Okay." I groped my way toward the computer desk.

"Even if you just want to use my computer, you're more than welcome. Here's my card." It said: *Moses Kellman, Ph.D., Professor Emeritus of English*. It was subtle, but I think what he was trying to hint at was that *he really would like another visit*.

I settled into a swivel chair wrapped in hockey tape and glanced at the spindly ficus tree next to the window. The microwave beeped in the kitchen while I waited for my email account to open.

I stared at the inbox of my new anonymous email address. Something was wrong.

There were three messages from Tamara and one from Jeremy. That wasn't unusual. But there were another eleven letters from people I'd never heard of.

I scanned the names. Daniel? Rebecca? Deb? Who were these people? Only Tamara and Jeremy knew this brand new address and the reason for it. This didn't seem right. My spam filter must have stopped working.

I opened a message and read it. My hands gripped the armrests and I let out a gasp. I looked at another message. And then another. I felt my eyes growing like inflating balloons. I read every one of those letters.

This wasn't spam. These emails all had one thing in common.

Every one of these people was asking me to set them up.

chapter 8

→ Bubby, I Got Problems ←

It had to be a mistake. How had these people found me? Did
they know who I was? Had Tamara and Jeremy told all their
friends about me? Tamara had asked if I knew anyone for her
friend Rebecca, but I figured it was just a compliment. Or a
joke.

> Dear Matchmaven,
> I'm hoping that you can help me. I've had such an awful
> time getting dates. I'm twenty-nine years old, attended the
> University of Toronto and now work as an occupational
> therapist. I'd love to find an observant guy who volunteers
> and values contributing to others' lives. I volunteer for

Jewish Helping Hands. I'm five-foot-five, with brown hair and brown eyes. I got your email address from Tamara (what can I say — that girl doesn't know how to say no) and I understand that you work anonymously. I'm incredibly frustrated and down from my dating situation. (Or lack of therewith.) Will you please, please, help me?

Deb Cohen

Thanks a lot, Tamara! Everyone must have believed Matchmaven was capable of performing dating miracles, because each letter was soaked in sadness.

Dear Matchmaven,

I heard you're like a miracle worker from my cousin Rebecca. I've had such a rough time finding my soul mate. I get a bit nervous on dates. What's really embarrassing is that I start sweating and after an hour my clothes are soaking. I know that sounds gross. I've actually brought a spare set of clothing in my car so I could secretly run out and change during the date. The first time I did that, I accidentally brought different clothes, and when I came back to the table the girl gave me a funny look. Which made me even more nervous. I think I'm a nice guy though. I'm decent looking, and successful as a chartered accountant. I own my own house. I love my nieces and nephews. I'm really most comfortable with kids — I love them. And my dog. I have a Great Dane named Bronx. We run together every day. Bronx and I visit two elderly blind men every week.

I'm thirty years old and looking for a great girl who wants to keep a kosher home. Do you think you could help me?

Thanks, Daniel Sharfstein

Hi Matchmaven,

Can you help me? My old friend Daniel Sharfstein said amazing things about you. I'm a 34-year-old dental hygienist and love singing in a women's choir. I enjoy historical fiction, philosophy, and current events.

I'm also slightly OCD. I'm extremely picky about my food. I have this thing where I prefer eating cold colour foods to warm colour ones. I haven't had ketchup for years since Heinz stopped making it in green and purple. For some reason, guys seem to get freaked out by this. I'm a giving person and am anxious to find a match. I heard you've done some great work and am hoping that you can help me find a great Jewish husband.

Shelly Sarfati

Were these people *insane*? Me? A matchmaker?

Hello, I was a sixteen-year-old stranger in a *really* strange land. (We're talking about a city that worships a hockey team that hasn't won a championship since the Vietnam war.) I didn't even have my own computer. What did I know about matchmaking? And why were they all turning to *me*?

This had to be a mistake. I typed in a message.

Dear Tamara,

We need to talk!

Rain

No, on second thought this couldn't wait for an answer. I needed to speak to Tamara immediately.

I swivelled the chair and called out. "Professor Kellman, can I please use your phone?"

"Sure, right there on the end table." I picked up the receiver of the old rotary phone to call Tamara. This was no simple matter since dialling a number on those things can run you back ten minutes or so. I was glad I had her number memorized. There was no answer on her line so I left her a message that I needed to speak to her immediately.

I shuffled back to the kitchen, still reeling from the emails. "Professor Kellman, I think I need to go now."

"You sure?"

I traipsed back to the computer to log out of my account just as another email came in.

Hi Matchmaven,

I'm hoping you can help me. I'm 23 years old and I just moved from New York to go to nursing school in Toronto. I was engaged to be married next month, but my fiancé Ben broke it off.

My entire body froze.

Our relationship wasn't perfect. I knew that Ben had some hesitations but my younger sister got into trouble at school with an elderly teacher and that was the final straw for him. Let's just say that she's somewhat irresponsible. Unfortunately my parents coddled her and didn't impose any consequences on her. On top of that she was sent to Toronto, where Ben and I were supposed to be starting out. Ben said he was completely turned off of my family and it confirmed his doubts about our relationship. Now I'm stuck in Toronto because I'm enrolled in a Bachelor of Nursing program here. Anyway, I'm 5-foot-6, slender, with

black hair and blue eyes. I also work at a hospice in down-
town Toronto. I love cooking and I'm a runner. I've been
volunteering with my aunt at an abused women's shelter. I
think that I'd like to be a midwife one day.

Can you help me?

Thanks so much!

Leah Resnick

My heart raced. I said my goodbye to Professor K. and
stumbled out to the front porch where the last of the day's sun
was tucking itself into the horizon for the night.

In a daze I drove back to the Bernsteins', my brain a complete mess.

It really was my fault.

So that's why no one would talk to me. I felt sick. I had an
overwhelming need to speak to my mother. I staggered into
the Bernsteins' house and noticed MazelTovNation was open
on the computer monitor. That was obviously the last thing
Leah had looked at on the computer before she left home. My
hands shook as I hung Uncle Eli's car key on the wall hook.
Would Leah hate me even more if she knew that I was the
Matchmaven she had opened up to? The worst part was that I
couldn't even apologize to her. My family was trying to protect
me . . . from me.

I glanced at my watch and calculated the time difference
between Toronto and Hong Kong. I climbed the stairs to my
bedroom and kicked off my shoes. Curling up on my bed I
dialled my mother's number. No answer.

My father wasn't there either and of course I wasn't allowed
to call my best friends in New York, Maya or Danielle. There
was too much of a risk of Aunt Mira checking the call log if I

tried it. For someone who was completely on top of my social game at Maimonides a few months ago, I felt utterly alone. The girls here were so reserved and unfriendly. The thought of nine more wretched months in this city made my eyes begin to sting.

I pulled out the pink Post-its.

Things I miss about New York:
~ friends (waaaaaaaa)
~ Manhattan
~ knishes
~ seltzer
~ everyone there knows what seltzer is

Although I knew I should have been studying, I wandered downstairs and tried to call my parents again. They still weren't answering and my gloom was deepening by the minute. Bubby Bayla sat knitting silently in the recliner in the family room. I plunked myself down on the leather couch and stared out the window to the park. Three teenage girls lounged on a picnic bench under the gazebo, laughing and chatting. A dull ache throbbed in my chest.

I glanced at Bubby in the recliner — she'd have to do.

"Bubby, I got problems."

She put down her knitting in her lap and peered at me through her thick cat glasses. Taking this as an invitation, I launched into a rant.

"Jeremy was supposed to be this great match for my sister, but I didn't know and I fixed him up with this really nice girl, Tamara, and they seem to be crazy about each other, but I can't tell anyone because Aunt Mira and Leah really wanted

Jeremy to go out with her and now they're going to be so mad when they find out that I fixed them up and Leah will get even angrier at me, since it's my fault that her engagement is broken. And Mom will be upset with me — again. Oh, and Mrs. Levine hates me and the girls are really unfriendly here and I'm terrified that if I mess up I'll have to go back to my parents in Hong Kong and finish high school by correspondence."

I couldn't believe that I unburdened myself to somebody who had hairs growing out of her chin.

"Let's get some pizza," she said, dropping her knitting into the fabric bag at her feet.

I stared at her in awe. Until five minutes ago it didn't even occur to me that she had teeth.

"You can do that?"

"Don't be ridiculous. Go get my purse. It has my credit card." She picked up the phone from the side table and dialled the pizza place number by heart, ordering a large olive pizza, two spicy fries, and a large Diet Coke.

She was one efficient Bubby.

Bubby's eyes flitted to her watch. "Just go pick up the food — it'll be faster."

Thirty minutes later I returned from Café Mango, carrying a pizza box with a large paper bag. I placed the pizza on the table where Bubby had set out plates, glasses, napkins, and a large bottle of ketchup. She sat at the head of the table and I dropped into the seat next to her as she pulled out the french fry containers from the brown paper bag.

"So you're the one who fixed up Jeremy?" she said in a loud voice.

"I am so dead," I said as I opened the pizza box, releasing the melted cheese and tomato sauce vapours into the kitchen air.

"Nah," she said as she squirted a small puddle of ketchup onto her plate. "Just don't blab."

I pulled back in my chair. "What? Not tell Aunt Mira?"

"Oh please," Bubby said, popping a fry in her mouth. "I'm going to tell you something but first go to the fridge. I need a beer."

I obeyed immediately. "But Mira always seems to know everything," I said as I opened the stainless steel door. Leaning into a cloud of cold air I rooted through the fridge until I found a chilly bottle of Corona.

"Don't forget the lime," Bubby called out.

I returned to the table, handed the bottle to Bubby, and slid into the seat next to her. She took a long swig and wiped her mouth with the back of her hand. She curled her bony finger, beckoning me to move closer. I leaned in until our faces were three inches away from each other, the whiff of beer tickling my nose. "Between you, me, and the lamppost, there's something you need to know about my daughter-in-law Mira."

"Really? What?"

Her eyes flicked around the kitchen and she lowered her voice to a conspiratorial whisper. "She's a *tyrant.*"

I blinked. "Huh?"

Bubby grabbed my arm and squeezed. "She's a *control freak.*" She pinched her lips together, nodded, and leaned back in her chair, satisfied as she savoured my reaction to this delectable info-gem she had just gifted to me. Before I had the chance to question her, the front door burst open and the sound of clomping drew closer to the kitchen.

Mira entered the kitchen with my sister trailing behind her. Mira glared at me, then slammed her briefcase onto the kitchen table. "Rain!"

Bubby shot me a knowing look.

Unease prickled me. Mira turned to me, hands on her hips. "Did I *not* ask you to deliver a dinner after school today?"

"Yes," I said cowering. "I took it over. There was no problem."

Her nostrils flared. "Well, there *is* a problem."

Leah reached out and lightly cupped my aunt's arm, her brows knitted with worry. I'm not sure what scared me more, Mira's wrath or Leah's disappointment. "I took it, I swear," I said in a feeble voice.

"Then why did the family just call me asking where their dinner was?"

"What? I took all the foil pans in the fridge right to the house — 141 Magnolia Drive!"

She took a deep cleansing breath and then said in her Very. Controlled. Voice. "It was 141 *Gladiola* Drive. You took the meal to the wrong house."

chapter 9
The Colour of Squirrel

"You took a shiva meal to the wrong family?" Bubby smacked her fist on the table. "I never even *heard* of anyone doing that. And I'm old!" She threw her head back and roared with laughter.

My purse sat on one of the kitchen chairs. I unzipped it and yanked out Professor Kellman's business card. "I took it to this nice old professor," I said, trying to steady my voice. "His wife died. He told me."

Aunt Mira looked at the card for a few seconds and handed it back to me. "Mo Kellman lost his wife ten years ago."

"Does that mean the shiva is over?"

Aunt Mira glared at me, then suddenly noticed the spread on the table.

She pointed to the box of partially eaten pizza and the french fry containers. "What's this?" she said in a pinched voice.

"Um. Dinner," I said.

She turned to Bubby Bayla. "Ma. Please tell me that you didn't have any pizza."

Bubby shrugged slowly and looked down at the table, affecting a faux innocent pose. A Golden Globe—winning performance it was not.

Mira's face hardened as she turned to me. "How did this food get here?"

"I . . . drove Uncle Eli's car to pick it up."

"*You* brought this food here?" she said, her face red. "My mother-in-law is on a salt-restricted diet. This kind of food is extremely dangerous for her."

I blanched. And no, in case you're wondering, I did not rat out Bubby for this culinary set-up.

"Well, I have a huge problem," Mira said. "Do you have *any* idea how embarrassing it is that the Millers didn't get their dinner?"

"I'm really sorry, I —"

Her hands shot up in the air and she squeezed her eyes shut: the variation of covering one's ears that is more socially accepted in middle-aged circles.

Leah spoke in a quiet voice. "Aunt Mira, I really wish you would have let me take care of it."

"Me too," Mira said.

Ouch.

Bubby was chuckling. My non-shiva visit had apparently given her a new lease on life. Leah put her hand on Mira's arm and spoke in a calming voice. "Why don't I go to Café

Mango and pick up some pies and salads. I'm happy to take them over to the Millers."

Mira exhaled slowly while she considered it. "Fine," she finally said with a nod. Leah shook her head at me and strode past me to the wall hook where she grabbed the car keys.

"I think I better come along to the Millers," said Aunt Mira. "I'd like to apologize in person."

They swept out the door, leaving me standing alone in the kitchen with Bubby.

"See what I mean?" she said. "A *tyrant*."

Then she plucked a french fry from the box and popped it into her mouth.

The next day I found myself once again trapped in Mrs. Levine's weekly torture session. I stared at a photo of her grinning granddaughter in a sticky high chair with spaghetti falling off every surface. It looked like the girl's head had been hand-dipped in a fondue dish of tomato sauce. The unfinished pine frame was painted with messy childish hearts, the words "I Luv You — Miriam" crudely written on the bottom.

Really? Or was this just one of those coercive "I Love You" craft projects that preschools foist on defenseless grandchildren?

Mrs. Levine's clipped voice jarred me back to reality. "I'm going to suggest you try to spend some time with someone responsible in the school. Someone like Dahlia Engel, perhaps. Do you know her?"

Of course I knew Dahlia Engel. She was the class brain with hair the colour of squirrel.

"Your aunt and I had a long talk this morning," Mrs. Levine was saying. I already didn't like where this was going. "We're both concerned about your lack of social integration at Moriah, and we think Dahlia would be an excellent mentor for you. She'll help you with your studying and to develop some friendships with the other students."

That was it. I was going to have to strangle Mira.

My hands clenched the moulded edges of my seat. "Mrs. Levine, are you sure you don't want to give me a bit more of a chance to connect on my own with some of the girls here?" Like girls I actually wanted to be friends with?

"Your second math test as well as your English assignment were on the weak side. I don't want you to fall further behind, and I think sometimes it helps to have a friend."

Dahlia Engel?

Mrs. Levine stared at me without blinking.

Sharks. I thought of sharks. Did you know that sharks have upper and lower eyelids and *they don't blink either*?

I rest my case.

I shifted in my chair as she continued a blinkless glare. I had no choice but to agree. "Okay, Mrs. Levine," I mumbled as I stared down at my hands.

The meeting was over. Just like that.

I spent the afternoon fantasizing an escape back to New York. But every scenario ended with the same inevitable result — an eight-thousand-mile exile to my parents' apartment. When the afternoon was thankfully over I trudged to my locker through an end-of-the-day kaleidoscope of unbrushed hair, abandoned uniform sweaters, and discarded candy wrappers. The roar of yelling and laughter squeezed my head like a clamp. Nobody waved. No one even acknowledged me.

I was completely invisible.

Maybe I really did need the principal to set me up on a play date with Calculator Girl.

The next morning, Aunt Mira drove me to the bus stop.

"How *is* Mo doing?" Aunt Mira said as she turned onto Bathurst Street.

"Mo?"

"Professor Kellman. Moses."

"Oh," I said. "Sad."

She shook her head. "I was friends with his daughter Rena, before she moved to Lakewood with her family," she said. "Now he's all alone."

"He appreciated the meal," I said. And since I was now in the business of winning points I added, "And I think he appreciated the visit too."

"Really?" She leaned over and squeezed my wrist. "He enjoyed chatting with you?"

"He practically *begged* me to come back," I said proudly.

"You don't say," she said in an intrigued voice. She drove quietly for a few seconds, then smacked the steering wheel with excitement. "I have a wonderful idea," she said. "Since he wants you to come back, you'll take another meal over and then you can visit with him again!"

"What?" As in: *What . . . have I done?!*

"I'm sure he'll be delighted!" she said, as she cruised through the intersection.

So this is what it was like to be the victim of your own success. Although I admittedly didn't have much experience with it. It was just too awkward to visit a complete stranger. What would I talk to him about?

"Say, Wednesday?" she said. "I'll let him know that you'll bring over some dinner."

I gritted my teeth as she dropped me off at the Number 7 bus stop. I stamped up the stairs of the bus looking for Tamara.

Tamara was at the back of the bus in her usual place, practically dancing in her seat. "I just know it," she said. "I'm afraid to get excited but I think Jeremy is The One."

Alright, in case you're thinking this is bizarre, here are a few other things you should know:

> *More Rules for Dating in My Community*
> #4. It's possible to know as early as the first
> date that the match is going to work.
> #5. It's not unheard of to get engaged within
> a week or two of meeting each other.
> #6. Dating has one purpose and one ulti-
> mate prize — marriage.

Okay, so I know Number 5 sounds *really* crazy but my mother has seen it happen many times in her matchmaking experience. People meet and know right away that they've found their soul mates.

"This is so great," I said to Tamara. Her eyes were dancing and a huge dippy grin spread across her delicate face. It had been a while since I'd earned a smile like that. From anyone.

"Let's get together," she said. "Should we try the library again?"

"Well . . ." I said. "How would you feel about getting together at this professor's house on Wednesday?" Fortified by Tamara, the visit to the professor might not be as awkward. "I'm delivering a meal for my aunt and I'd appreciate having someone else there to talk to him. Plus he doesn't mind me using his computer. I can start responding to all those people who are asking for matches." With that I gave her a knowing nudge.

"I'm still so sorry that happened," she said with a sober expression. "Rebecca begged me for Matchmaven's email address. She swore she wouldn't tell anyone."

I shrugged. It was too late now. "Don't worry about it," I said. "The email account is anonymous."

"Absolutely. Now just tell me where to go."

"Wednesday night," I said, scribbling Professor Kellman's address on the back of my transfer.

"Wednesday night it is," she said as she pocketed the number. She pointed to my knapsack. "Now it's time for some math."

I groaned and pulled out my textbook.

chapter 10

Looks like George Clooney

Professor K. clapped his hands together and grinned at us.

"Come in, come in," he said. "I'm delighted you're here."
He wore a zippered black cardigan over an ash-coloured shirt
that looked oddly stylish on his older frame. Though slightly
confusing, these kinds of happy fashion accidents are known
to randomly occur.

"I can't believe I forgot to bring a flashlight," I whispered
to Tamara as we followed him to the tiny kitchen. I placed the
aluminum pan filled with slices of roast beef and baked potatoes on the laminate counter.

He lifted the foil and sniffed the contents. "Delicious.
Your Aunt Mira is a wonderful cook." He pointed to the vinyl

chairs. "Please, sit, sit. Would you like some fresh juice? I have a juicer. I insist."

Tamara smiled at him. "Thank you. That would be lovely."

"What'll it be then?" he said. "Celery? Kohlrabi?"

I stifled a groan. "Do you maybe have some oranges?"

"Carrots, I'll make you some nice orange carrot juice."

Why? Why the resistance to fruit?

He scurried to the fridge, bent down, and pulled out an unrecognizable vegetable.

"Who's your friend?" he asked, peering over his shoulder.

She looked down at him. "I'm Tamara Greenberg."

"Of course," he said, smiling.

As he fed the vegetables through the juicer, I leaned over the table to Tamara.

"Sooo?" I said to her.

Tamara rested her face in her hands; elbows on the table. Her green eyes were so luminous they looked like they were powered by an internal battery pack. She had an air of contentment — she radiated marriage. "Honestly, Rain? I feel that we're destined to spend the rest of our lives together."

I could probably do a cartwheel of awesome right now, except for two things. And they were both guilt. The fact was that Leah was languishing and not dating. And the tension between us was slowly gnawing its way through me.

"Well, ladies, I have some delicious juice for you," Professor K. said.

He handed me a glass filled with a strange slimy substance. It wasn't really clear to me if it was liquid or gas. I can tell you this much though. If you bottled the sweaty air on a sealed Number 7 bus, you'd almost certainly get something that looked like the contents of this glass. I needed a diversion because there was no way I was going to actually put that stuff inside my body.

"Hey Professor K., did you write all those books in your living room?" I asked. I gently shook the glass, swirling the contents.

"One or two," he said. "Would you like to see some of my work?"

We marched single file to the living room, and what followed was a guided tour of Planet Kellman. I shot a glance at the droopy ficus plant that stood near a tiny crack of light next to the brown velour drapes. I inched over and furtively dumped the bio-concoction in the soil. As Professor K. continued pointing out books to Tamara that were penned by his late wife, I settled into the taped-up seat in front of his computer and opened my email account.

It had happened again. Messages from another twelve people requesting matches filled my inbox.

Tamara sidled over and glanced over my shoulder. "Wow. Maybe just set up an automatic response that you're not doing matches."

I crossed my arms and stared at the screen. My legend was growing by the day. That's because they didn't know that as many people as I had brought together (two), I had broken up (two). In fact, maybe Tamara was a fluke. Her cell phone rang. As she yanked it from her purse, Professor K. wandered to the kitchen.

"Anybody want a tea?" he asked.

"No thanks," I said, not so interested in risking a zucchini or broccoli blend. I opened another message.

Dear Matchmaven,

I've heard amazing things about you and I'm hoping you

can help me. I'm thirty-two and a paralegal. I'm physically
fit, have a great relationship with my family and friends,
am a fantastic baker, and spend a lot of time helping out
my elderly grandfather. My friends say that I'm cute looking. I've had no luck with internet dating and I just don't
meet the right kind of men. Maven, I'm so ready to get
married. Is it too late for me to find Mr. Right and actually have a family? I want it so badly. Can you help me?
Thanks so much,
Ilana Rosenthal

Tamara reappeared in the living room, leaning into her
cell phone, deep in conversation. Jeremy, obviously. Professor
K. puttered around the kitchen, seemingly happy just to have
people in his house.

"You already got the flight reservations?" she asked, as she
dropped onto the plastic-encased couch.

I opened up the next email.

Dear Matchmaven,

I'm looking for a highly intelligent woman under the age of
thirty who is accomplished, gorgeous, modest, kind, giving,
financially stable, has a good relationship with her parents,
is supportive, volunteers, is well travelled, reads, enjoys
the theatre and fine kosher dining. She must love children,
be outgoing, have a good sense of humour, and want to
have a large family. Oh, and walks on the beach too. I'm a
consultant who looks like George Clooney.
Jonathan Sandler

Was George asking *me* out?

"I'll call my parents right away to let them know that we're coming," Tamara was saying.

I looked up. Tamara was biting her lower lip and nodding vigorously. Her eyes shone and she rocked side-to-side in a kind of couch jig as she breathed into her phone. I mouthed, "What's up?" and Tamara pointed to the empty ring finger on her left hand, then crossed her fingers and grinned. I hooted and patted her on her shoulder. It sounded like a proposal was in the pipes! The scent of chamomile announced Professor K.'s return to the living room. He shuffled into the dining room and sat down.

"I think she finally may have met the man of her dreams," I murmured.

"Okay, Jeremy," Tamara said. "Talk to you later."

After a brief pause, she said, "Me too," in a soft voice and then hung up.

I grasped the plastic arms of the desk chair and rolled forward. "Sooo . . ." I said.

"Jeremy wants to go out to Vancouver on Sunday to meet my family!" she yelped and then lowered her voice. "This sounds *very* promising. I think he's going to propose!" I flew to the couch and grabbed her in a bear hug. "My fingers are crossed too," I said.

Professor K. clapped his hands with delight.

Now that he was part of the inner circle, of course.

chapter 11
→→→ I'm Not Exactly a Dog ←←←

While Tamara and Jeremy were off in Vancouver, the emails kept rolling in.

> Dear Matchmaven,
>
> I heard that you can do amazing matches for people in the community. I'm so frustrated I simply don't know what to do anymore. I'm a thirty-nine-year-old pediatric surgeon who also does cellular research and have published in numerous journals. I love children and enjoy helping people; I volunteer as a medical clown for the kids in the hospital. I'm no movie star but I'm not exactly a dog either.

Maven, you cannot believe how awful I present on dates. I get so nervous I'm reduced to a puddle of terror and laugh in a weird and crazy way. I don't have time to meet anyone on my own and I could use some tips on how to do this right. I'm dying to get married to a girl who keeps kosher and Shabbos.

Could you help me?

Best regards,

Reuben Kahn

I began to consider sending out a form email out announcing my resignation. I mean, it was a short and meteoric career with a 100 percent success rate after all, so why not retire on a high note?

But it was the next one that made something catch in my throat.

Dear Matchmaven,

I haven't heard from you so I thought I'd give it another shot. I'm a little worried that my last email to you was a bit on the negative side. My fiancé broke off our engagement two months before the wedding. And then I was disappointed when this really cute lawyer who hangs out at my aunt's house started going out with someone else, and now they're serious.

Matchmaven, I'm feeling so awful. I'll be honest — I'm considered on the pretty side. I can be an incredibly loyal and loving friend. My family is great. Even my immature sister can be sweet sometimes. I'm so incredibly lonely and hopeless now and wondering if I'll ever get married and have a family.

I closed my eyes and willed my heartbeat to slow down to a reasonable rate.

The pain of Leah's description of me ("immature") was overshadowed by her affirmation of me ("sweet"), which was overshadowed by her misery ("hopeless").

What we had here was an extra-large serving of over-shadows. I had caused her even more despair by bringing Jeremy and Tamara together. I racked my brain, wondering who else would have the influence to get Ben to give Leah another chance, but I came up blank.

An achy feeling tugged on my stomach. I had no choice in the matter.

Ben was over and done with and now I was going to have to use all these emails for Leah's benefit. I was going to find Leah a husband!

And I mean really. How hard could it be to make another match?

Okay, I take that back. It was impossible to make a match. I didn't even know how to begin. All thoughts of homework or review completely vanished as I attempted to sort through the matchmaking requests. At 10 p.m. I was still sitting at my desk poring over the emails but my cell phone just wasn't sufficient for the task.

I bounced downstairs to the empty kitchen to check out the privacy situation. Glancing at the hospice schedule hanging on the wall, I got good news. Leah was on a shift. Mira, Eli, and Bubby were all in bed for the night. Perfect.

I plopped down at the desk, my hope booting up the computer.

The first thing I did was open MazelTovNation. Nothing new was doing there.

The next step was to scan the roster of emails in Match-maven's inbox. Somewhere in this list of letters was a dyna-mite man, searching for his Leah Resnick. I may have blown it with Ben, but I now had a second chance.

I scrolled through the messages and counted thirty-three people. I set up a table in Word with separate columns for men (nineteen), women (fourteen), age, and preferences.

I wasn't quite sure of what to do next. There were ten men in their mid to late twenties. Excellent. I carefully examined their letters. Were they financially stable? Polished? Good-looking? Normal?

I considered establishing a Nerd Index for the really chal-lenging cases from a scale of one to five. A one would go to a person who appeared normal and had only slightly annoy-ing habits like inappropriate laughter. A five would apply to someone with mastery of Klingon or an addiction to the Weather Channel.

I studied the emails of the ten men but without CliffsNotes to interpret what they were *really* saying, I wasn't certain what kind of people they were. If someone describes himself as good-looking, is that less reliable than "others say that I'm good-looking"? It seemed that more of the men were con-cerned with physical appearances than women. Was that a coincidence?

Aaron was a math person, so he and Leah had the sciencey

thing in common. She'd done her first undergraduate degree in chemistry, thinking she'd become a pharmacist, but decided that she preferred working directly with patients. Daniel was quirky, but he sounded solid. There really wasn't an ideal mate for Leah. She was fragile now. One bad date and she'd be more discouraged. Can you really take two less ideally matched people and make it work? Maybe Tamara and Jeremy really were just a lucky accident. Most people present themselves as perfect, although my clients, for whatever reasons, trusted me with their flaws.

That's when I got the idea.

I'd do a practice match! Try to assist some of the souls who were begging for my help. And then I'd really know what I was doing. Two names jumped out at me, Ilana and George Clooney. He was a real catch. At thirty-two, she was slightly older than his preferred age range, but I didn't think it was that important. She was cute and he was good-looking. She was close with her grandfather and was a giving person.

I clicked onto George's email again and it definitely looked like a match. My mom always said that some people had the knack for making a match, and it looked like I might possibly be one of those people after all.

"What are you doing?" a voice said behind my shoulder.

I spun around in my chair. Leah stood behind me in a grey sweat top and a long slinky skirt that hugged her slender frame.

"I, I, I'm working on a paper." My heart pounded as I maniacally tapped the sign-out button on the Matchmaven account. "I thought you were at work at the hospice."

"I changed shifts," she said. "Can I get the computer for a second? I need the printer."

"Sure." I nodded. "Let me just exit."

The email account finally closed, bringing up MazelTov-Nation. I glanced at the most recent announcements.

Jeremy Koenig and Tamara Greenberg were engaged!

"Yes!" I said as I punched the air.

It was too late. Leah's face fell. "I didn't know you were so close to Jeremy." My mouth gaped open. Think fast!

"He just seems. I don't know. Um, lonely?"

Leah stared down at her hands.

"He's so nerdy, you know what I mean?" I babbled. "Like who was going to want to marry him? It seemed so hopeless."

"Then there really isn't much hope for the rest of us," she said in a quiet voice.

"But Leah you're so awesome —"

"Rain, don't."

I swallowed as I exited MazelTovNation and the Word document with the list of names popped up.

No time to save it anywhere. My heart pounded as I closed the document with all the work that went into it. If only I could have closed down all the mistakes that had brought me here.

Do you want to save the changes? it asked.

No, not really.

Not at all.

chapter 12

⋙⟶ A Loud Rap on the Door ⟵⋘

On Friday morning I bounded to the back of the bus, where Tamara waited for me in our usual seats. She threw her arms around me and squealed. Guilt was biting me, but celebration won out. I really was so happy for her.

"Congratulations, Tamara! *Mazel tov!*"

The Groomer, one of the bus regulars, stopped flossing.

"My friend's engaged — she's getting married!" I shouted to him. You know it's a pretty cool day when a guy with a foot of dental floss hanging from his mouth starts looking slightly charming.

"Do you have a ring?" I said to Tamara.

"Well, we have to —"

"Do you have a hall?"

"We think —"

"When are you getting married? *Talk fast*, my stop is coming."

Tamara laughed. "Right now all you have to know about is the engagement party. Monday night at the Harmonia."

I looked at my only friend as I leaned back in my seat. "I'm so excited, I can't believe this."

"I don't even know how to thank you," she said.

"You don't have to. I'm the second happiest person in the city today. Okay, maybe third after Jeremy."

She shook her head in wonder.

"How's the math going?" she said.

"It's not," I said, truthfully. In fact all of my studying had become obliterated by the overpowering Drive to Match.

"Oh and by the way, listen to this," Tamara said. "You went to Maimonides, right?"

"Let's talk about you, not me!"

"It's just that Aviva, you know that friend I mentioned who went there her senior year, is now *teaching* there —"

"That's not as interesting as you," I said. The back of my neck was starting to burn. "Tell me when the wedding's going to be and where!"

We talked wedding and my stop came too quickly. All morning, I wandered the school halls wired, running on a tank of *mazel tov*. I arrived in English class, full of matchmaking energy, ready to fill the world with love. I was giddy with excitement over tonight's date. After my emails, Jonathan and Ilana were going out and I had to be on call in case of any problems.

Today's class was in the computer lab where Miss Weiss was going to give us a lesson on online scholarly research. I charged through the room and planted myself in the distant corner as groups of chattering girls skipped through the room, claiming clusters of computers. (So they could compute communally, of course.) A blade of light escaped from a gap in the drapes and painted a stripe of heat down my back as I signed into my Matchmaven account.

Miss Weiss sat at the teaching computer, with the browser projected onto the tattered screen pinned to the wall.

"Everyone ready?" she said over the hum of the machines.

A loud rap on the door brought Miss Weiss to her feet. She pulled it open to reveal Mrs. Levine looming in the entrance.

That's the thing with Mrs. Levine, she didn't just stand — she loomed. And as loomers go, Mrs. Levine was a pro.

Mrs. Levine stepped inside and scanned the room until she cut her eyes on me and then whispered something to Miss Weiss. Miss Weiss bent down to Dahlia Engel, who was predictably sitting at the computer next to hers.

Dahlia gathered her papers in her knapsack and trudged back to the corner of the lab. My cheeks tingled as she dropped into the seat next to me, rolling her eyes. Shira and Natalie watched the sequence from the other side of the bank of computers, giving each other knowing looks.

"Can I help you with your searching?" Dahlia said, her voice like ice.

"Nope. I'm good," I said, rolling my eyes. With huge gold-framed glasses and shoes that looked like they'd been sitting on the shelves of Value Village the last two years, Dahlia was your garden variety brainiac. You just knew that if she had a pet it would be an *educational* animal like a snake. Or a gecko.

"Miss Weiss said that you'd probably need help," she said, rolling her eyes again. "I really don't mind."

"Actually, you could let Mrs. Levine know that I'm pretty good on the computer. In fact, do you need my help?" I said, rolling my eyes in response.

There was so much eye-rolling going on between the two of us that pretty soon we'd have to move this conversation over to the waiting room of the nearest ophthalmologist. Dahlia must have had the same concern because we switched to scowling and after a full minute of mutual glaring we established a silent pact to ignore each other.

I returned to Matchmaven where there was an email from Jonathan.

> Hey Matchmaven,
>
> Thanks so much for setting me up with Ilana — can't wait to meet her. I'm so sorry to do this but I have a midnight flight to Chicago, so I need to move the date up an hour earlier. Can you let Ilana know that I'll pick her up at 7:00? Otherwise we'll have to leave it until I'm back in town. Let me know as soon as you can, since I'll be offline all day.
>
> Thanks so much,
>
> Jonathan Sandler

I emailed back. No problem.

Unfortunately however, there *was* a problem. Ilana's email bounced back with an automatic, "out of office" message. The string of emails between us was generated from her work address.

I emailed Jonathan but he was out of reach already. I examined Ilana's email, which had her contact information, including her cell phone number, on the bottom. I had no choice so I texted her with the update.

Me: Matchmaven here. Change of time. Jonathan's picking
you up at 7.
Ilana: Can't wait! Thanks for your help, Maven.
Me: Good luck!

Mrs. Weiss was at her computer, showing the class something about library databases. Checking my inbox was becoming an obsession now that I had a mission to match Leah, so
I peeked again and noticed another email. This one was a
thirty-three-year-old female with a penchant for risk-taking.
(*"I need someone who really gets me. Like they should also enjoy off-trail skiing,
urban tree-climbing, and running up the down-escalator in department stores.
You see what I'm saying?"*)

Actually I didn't. I shook my head and much to my surprise heard Dahlia giggling. *She was reading my monitor.*

I glared at her. "Excuse me?"

"Are you like a matchmaker or something?"

My back went rigid; the muscles on my face taut.

Dahlia shrugged and returned to her computer.

My life was over. It was the way of the grapevine. Once
Dahlia exposed me, news would migrate and travel and eventually Leah would find out and feel that I'd been lying to her,
which I had been, but that's beside the point. She would never
ever trust me again.

I had to admit the obvious — I was an idiot for checking the
Matchmaven account in public. I could hardly blame her for
glancing at a huge desktop computer monitor that was positioned twelve inches from her face.

I can be so dumb. It was impossible for me to stay in the
room. I signed out of my email, threw my papers into my
knapsack, and lumbered to the front of the class.

"Miss Weiss, I feel really sick. Can I leave?"

"Of course."

I clomped down the corridor in search of some corner where I could crank up to maximum misery with minimum distraction.

Somebody was following me.

It was Dahlia. "What?" I said.

"Are you coming back to class?"

"No, Dahlia, I'm *done*, thank you very much," I said.

She stepped in front of me, blocking me, then folded her arms. "You *have* to come back. Like, immediately."

A shot of anger poked my chest. "Are you for real?" This is a person who took her babysitting responsibilities pretty seriously if she was now giving orders. "Do you have a problem?"

"Actually, I do. My *problem* is Mrs. Levine," Dahlia said.

"Why, you going to lose community service hours or something?"

"No. I'm just going to get called into her office — again — because I didn't help you. And I'll get harangued. Again."

"What are you talking about? You're the poster child for the Levine Educational Model."

Dahlia's stare hardened. "You just have no idea, do you?"

"Look, I don't know what your problem is. All I know is that she's constantly punishing me for being a bad person and a bad student."

"Well, she's constantly punishing me for being a *good* student."

"Huh?" I slid my knapsack strap off my shoulder, and let it drop between my feet.

"She wants me to 'be challenged,'" Dahlia said, making air quotes, "so she gives me extra work. And she thinks that if I 'mentor' you," more air quotes, "that it will solve my perceived social problems. She's trying to get me to connect with the new girl."

I rolled my eyes. "Like *I'm* supposed to help *you* make friends?" I was after all, completely invisible at Moriah. I waited to say more until a group of three girls had passed us to enter the bathroom door behind Dahlia. "That woman has made my life miserable since the day I got here." And of course, becoming immersed in matchmaking wasn't exactly having a positive impact on my grades.

"That's because she lives in this alternate universe where tormenting is an expression of caring," she said.

"Oh my god, exactly."

"Look," she said. "I'm sorry that I looked at your monitor."

I sighed.

She cocked her head to the side and peered at me. "Are you really a matchmaker?"

"It's a long story and it's very confidential."

"It's in the vault," Dahlia said as she zipped up her lips with her fingers.

"And I'm sorry that I fell asleep during your presentation," I said. "I was up all night worrying about stuff."

"I understand. Ancient Mesopotamia is so . . . 2000," she said.

"BCE, of course."

"Listen, if you want me to set up a spreadsheet for your matchmaking, I could do a little database, like those big singles' sites. Would that help?"

"I'm okay." Even though it was slightly tempting.

"Just please come back to class with me," she said. She shrugged and turned around. "I don't want to mess with the Law of Levine, if you don't mind."

chapter 13

⋙──→ A Date with Disaster ←──⋘

That night I knocked off a barely passable essay for history class in less than three hours, while ignoring the rest of my schoolwork. I still had to study for the math test but of course had saved the worst for last. Driven by my new mission I took a break and returned to the safety and privacy of my bedroom to scour the Matchmaven account for my clients.

Today's bounty was excellent — three guy emails. I now understood that it was all a numbers game. The more men I had, the better the choices for Leah. If tonight's date with Ilana and Jonathan showed promise then I could be fairly confident that I interpreted the emails accurately and I'd be ready to make the best possible choice for Leah.

I glanced at my watch. It was after 10 p.m. and I hadn't heard from either Jonathan or Ilana. That was a positive sign.

As I scrolled through the emails, I was startled by the sound of my phone ringing, a tragically rare occurrence these days.

"Hi," a whispery voice breathed into the phone.

"Hello? Who is this?"

There was a moment's hesitation. "Is this Matchmaven?" she said. "This is Ilana. You texted me today."

My chest constricted. *Was I insane?*

"I figured it was okay to call."

I smacked my hand on the desk. This woman could blow my cover.

"Ilana," I said, trying to keep my voice even. "I have to operate anonymously. You understand?"

"Totally. I swear I won't tell anyone who you are."

I exhaled slowly.

"Actually, who are you?" she said.

"I *really* need to be anonymous."

"Please don't worry. But Matchmaven, I have an emergency. I agonized before calling you, but I really didn't know what else to do. I'm so sorry."

My grip was so fierce I thought the phone would crack. "Where are you now?"

"We went for a walk in York Hill Park."

Why would he take her to the park in early November in the middle of the community where everyone could see them together? He might as well have taken her to Times Square.

"Please, I have to ask you," she said, her voice catching. "Do you mind telling me where you live? I'm *desperate*." Was that a sob I heard?

"Are you . . . okay?" I said, even though I knew where this was going.

"Please," she said. She was definitely crying.

I lowered my voice, hoping she wouldn't hear me properly. "I live on Michael Court."

"Yes! Finally some good news," she said. "We're right here near the gazebo."

"Really?" I scurried to the window at the end of the hallway and squinted out into the darkness.

The fact is, I spent years trying to slay my personal yentas. Okay, maybe not. I admit — it's been ages since I lost the war on curiosity.

"Can you see me?" she said. "I'm wearing a long scrunchy skirt and a grey plaid jacket."

It was almost impossible to discern her figure. The black park was dotted with balls of gauzy amber light that hung like tiny planets from the lampposts. These were more like show lights that had been muted through a Vaseline-covered lens.

"I'm on the bench just south of the gazebo," she said. I searched the darkness until I made out a woman's shape, illuminated by a blade of pale yellow light.

"I'm really sorry about this," she breathed into the phone. "I'm kind of frantic. My skirt ripped when we were swinging on the swings. I'm also freezing. I'm holding it together with my hand, and I'm so embarrassed. Could you please, please, please do me a huge favour and bring a skirt?"

I snorted. "I'm supposed to show up on your date and hand you a skirt?"

"No. You walk by. Leave a bag with the clothes in the Porta-Potty and then I go in right after and change. It's a bit gross but it'll just take two minutes." She had it all figured out.

"I'm not even sure we're the same size," I said.

"Size eight."

"Well, there you go, I'm size four."

There was silence on the line. "I don't know what to do," she said in a quivering voice.

I had never heard of anything like this. The matchmaker showing up during a date? Besides, I had this huge test, and hours of emails to sort through.

I glanced down at MathMethods and exhaled a loud and showy sigh. "Fine," I said.

What else could I say to a dating wardrobe disaster? "I'll take a look for a skirt in my house," I said. The donation bag behind Mira's door probably had something for Ilana.

"It doesn't matter what it looks like. And you have my word that I absolutely won't tell a soul who you are. Speaking of which, who are you?"

"I'll be there in five," I said, trying to coat my voice in lightness, as I ignored her question. Ilana's situation had just blown my anonymity.

She sighed on the other end of the line.

I could hear Uncle Eli and Leah chatting quietly in the den. I threw on a black hoodie and sweater, then stole into their bedroom where Aunt Mira's pile of clothes were folded inside a shopping bag behind her door, waiting to be donated. I snatched a stretchy skirt figuring that it was a one-size-fits-all garment. It was probably Bubby's at one time, but it didn't matter. It was so dark in the park, Jonathan wouldn't really notice.

With my Converse sneakers laced up, I cautiously descended the stairs, crept out the front door, edged around the side of the house, and sprinted past the greying pressure-treated gate at the back of the Bernstein's yard that opened onto York Hill

Park. As the pulse of crickets echoed across the grassy fields, I crunched across dried leaves layered on moist grass toward the park bench.

When Ilana saw me, she rose from the bench, clapped the palm of her hand on her chest, and released a slow breath. She was shorter than I'd imagined, so she'd probably have to roll up the waistband of the old skirt. Her black hair fell in waves past her shoulders and the black narrow glasses that rested on her angular face gave her an unconventional artsy-geeky kind of beauty. I nodded and walked toward the Porta-Potty but the door was locked.

Who uses these things? This was one of the new UFO models constructed entirely from titanium metal and produced by a company in Scandinavia. And in case you think that I'm some kind of an ardent Porta-Potty enthusiast, I picked up this information morsel from the Bernstein dinner table. I guess when your house backs onto a park these are the kinds of things you notice.

"Where's Jonathan?" I said in a low voice, as I walked back over to her.

Ilana pointed at the Porta-Potty. I handed her the plastic bag, lowered myself onto the cold wooden bench, and wrapped my hoodie tighter around myself.

She held the bag to her chest and gazed at me. "You're really an extraordinary person. I am *so* grateful."

Tell it to Leah. "So what's this Jonathan guy like?"

She swallowed. "He asked me if there's anything I can do about my hair," she said with quivering lips.

I shot up from the bench. "He what?"

She gulped back tears. "I don't think he even knows my name."

"I could smack him," I muttered, sinking back onto the bench. Had I really blown this match so badly? "I'm so sorry about this."

"Well, I did learn that he earns bonuses in the six figures, women are dying to date him, and his bosses at the bank love him."

"Ugh. Does he at least look like George Clooney?"

"Nooo." She pulled one skirt on over the other, and lowered her torn skirt from inside. When she was done she dropped back onto the bench, gathered her ample hair into a ponytail, and turned to me with an apologetic face. "I am *so* sorry about all of this. I asked him to take me home so I could change my clothes."

"And?"

"He actually . . . *refused*," she said, shaking her head. "He told me that it doesn't matter. Like it wouldn't make a difference to how I look."

"What a jerk," I muttered under my breath. I rubbed my arms; the temperature was dropping by the minute. "How long has he been in there?"

She glanced at her cell phone. "I called you ten minutes ago," she said. "And he'd already been in there for a while."

"Wait a minute. You're telling me he's been in the can for like what, half an hour?"

She put her glasses on and glanced at the Porta-Potty. "That sounds like a problem, doesn't it?"

"You probably should check up on him."

"It's a *date*." She looked at me with disbelief. "That's embarrassing."

"Well, what if he's trapped? Or passed out, or something?"

She twisted her fingers and gazed at the Porta-Potty. "Can't you do it?"

I put my hands on my waist. "How old did you say you were?"

"Okay, *fine*," she said, rising to her feet.

She sidled over to the Porta-Potty and tentatively knocked on the door.

There was no answer. Ilana rapped on the door with more force and there was still no response. I stood up and joined her outside the Porta-Potty.

"Are you okay?" she said to the metal wall of the bathroom.

A muffled sound rumbled inside.

"Jonathan, are you in there?" she shouted.

A strained voice emerged from inside the titanium cage. "I'm stuck. The door's jammed."

"Of course, I'd never do it," she whispered to me. "But I'm almost tempted to leave. Like now."

"I do have a ton of work to get done," I said.

"It's win-win."

"Help me," Jonathan said. "I can barely breathe in here, I can't take it." He sounded like a strangled sheep.

"Is he *crying*?" Ilana asked, her eyes two huge circles of surprise.

"I'm not crying," Jonathan blubbered.

"Let's try to force it open," I said. I raised my arms and hammered my fists against the door, but it didn't budge. It was titanium after all.

"No, no, no. We need something large that we can use like a battering ram," Ilana said.

"Excellent idea." I peered around me, looking for an appropriate stick. I glanced at the perimeter of the park and could see the light in the Bernsteins' den still on. It would probably make sense if I could go back to the house and grab one of Uncle Eli's tools, but I couldn't take the risk of getting caught.

We fanned out through the pine trees, crunching on pine needles, searching for an object that was light enough to lift but strong enough to force the door open.

"I got it," Ilana yelled from the blackness. She emerged from behind a mound dragging a large branch across the grass.

We picked it up at each end and hoisted it waist high. We swung it three times and on the third count bashed it against the door.

The door didn't budge.

"What do we do now?" Ilana said, biting her lower lip. "It must be *really* hot in there."

"How about we count to three," I said. "Then we run toward this thing, jump up *higher*, and try to bash it with the weight of our bodies."

She gave the Porta-Potty a doubtful look. "I don't know," she said. "But I guess we could try."

We stepped back twenty-five yards or so away from the door. On the count of three we raced to the Porta-Potty and hammered the trunk against the door. The door didn't open but the entire booth slowly tipped precariously backwards. Ilana's mouth opened wide in horror as it teetered back. Jonathan yelped from inside. For a couple of seconds it looked like the structure would fall over, releasing gallons of raw sewage all over the cage — and Jonathan. I held my breath as the tiny box shuddered, trying to make up its mind. The Porta-Potty finally settled back in its upright position with a thud. It was a few seconds before my heart slowed down to a regular beat.

"I told you, I'm not crying," Jonathan sobbed.

"That's it," Ilana said. "I'm looking up the city's number. It's got to be awful in there." She grabbed the phone from her jacket pocket and wandered over to the bench. I stood guard next to the Porta-Potty, unsure of what to do next. A septic, chemical smell seeped out of a vent on top.

"Jonathan, don't worry, we'll get you out of here," I lied.

I glanced at my watch. It was 10:45, and I had around eighty hours of homework. I returned to the park bench to say goodbye just as Ilana got off her phone.

"Public Works is coming in fifteen minutes and they said to wait," she said as she dropped onto the bench.

Excellent. I was going home now.

"I'm so grateful you're not going home now," she said.

"I wouldn't even think of going home now," I answered.

We chatted for thirty minutes until a black flatbed truck motored up the walkway and came to a stop next to the gazebo. Two burly city employees wearing night reflective vests jumped out of the cab. The one wearing a black toque with a Toronto Raptors insignia on it grabbed a red metal tool kit from the back of the truck.

"Okay," he said. "Where's your friend, ladies?"

Ilana pointed to the bathroom. Raptors strode to the toilet and pulled out a screwdriver from his tool box. As he began to jimmy the lock I turned to leave. Finally.

"Rain, thank you so much for staying," Ilana said quietly. "I'd feel so awkward being alone with these two guys."

"Please," I said. "I wouldn't even *think* of going home now."

The other city employee had a thin grey ponytail under his black baseball cap. He watched Raptors struggling with the lock then returned to the truck to retrieve a crowbar.

Ilana narrowed her eyes and folded her arms across her

chest. "Can't you just use a drill to cut open the door?" she said to Ponytail.

"Are you kidding?" he said. He smacked the side of the Porta-Potty with an admiring gaze. "Nothing gets through these babies. They're built out of solid steel."

Jonathan banged on the inside of the unit. "Get me out of here. *Now*. Get this thing open, already."

Ponytail tried prying open the door with the crowbar without any luck. He turned to Raptors. "It's like . . . a malfunction! Can you believe this?"

"Never seen anything like it."

"We need to take it back to the shop," Ponytail said.

"You're right," Raptors said. "We can leave it for the boys to fix in the morning."

"No! Don't leave me, I'm dying."

"Okay," Ponytail said. "We'll bring it to the shop and try a chainsaw."

"Ilana," Jonathan cried from inside the Porta-Potty. "Please don't leave me."

"He's right, he shouldn't go alone," I said. What would happen if these men just left him there all night?

"Thank you, Rain. I was worried that I'd have to go alone. You're a sweetie."

Before I had a chance to protest, the men began moving the structure. They tipped it enough to load the Porta-Potty onto a dolly, secured it with strapping, and lowered a ramp from the flatbed. Then they gingerly pulled the structure onto the truck where they secured it with rope.

"You have a car?" Raptors said.

Ilana and I both shook our heads no.

He looked at Ponytail for an instant.

"Well, maybe you guys should ride in the back of the truck with him. We don't usually transport these things when they're . . . occupied."

I rolled my eyes and Ilana scrunched her face up and mouthed the words, "I'm sorry." Once Jonathan's bathroom was secured with a series of ropes to the truck, Ilana and I climbed on to the back and eased ourselves down on the cold metal. The truck slowly wended its way through the walkway, while Jonathan shuddered under the straps and cords.

We heard a moan. "It's sloshing in here."

Ilana shook her head. As the truck slowly rumbled through the park onto the street, I leaned against the rear window of the cab and gazed upward. It was a clear night and the full moon was so bright and low it looked like a wayward planet that had accidentally fallen out of the sky.

And was about to crash on my head — a great big ball of disaster.

A *date* with disaster, to be exact. And it was my entire fault. My success with Tamara and Jeremy had come too easily for me to fully grasp how tricky it was to make a match.

"Are we there yet?" Jonathan's voice came from inside the Porta-Potty. We were barely out of the park. I looked up again with a sigh. The moon was so completely in your face it was impossible to ignore.

Ilana must have been thinking the same thing. She leaned back on her elbows and gazed up at the sky like she was moon bathing. "Incredible, huh?" she said.

"My dad loves talking about Apollo 11," I said.

"Nineteen seventy-five must have been an amazing time," she said.

A hollow voice floated out of the bathroom. "It wasn't 1975."

"Um, I think I know what I'm talking about," Ilana said with a snort to the Porta-Potty. She turned to me. "My parents used to talk about it all the time."

"Don't you think I know the year of my bar mitzvah?" Jonathan said with irritation.

"What?" I said. I could not have possibly heard him correctly.

"Never mind," Jonathan said. "Just talking to myself. It's the fumes."

"Ilana," I whispered, my eyes bulging. "My grandfather died the year they landed on the moon and that was the year *my father* had his bar mitzvah."

"How old is your father?" she asked in a tight voice.

I gulped. "Fifty-eight."

Ilana and I looked at each other, our faces frozen in shock.

"Oh my god," Ilana said in a horrified whisper. "Jonathan is fifty-eight years old."

Ilana and I both shuddered.

She looked like she was going to throw up. "That is so gross."

"What difference does it make?" the indignant voice echoed from the Porta-Potty. "You didn't think I looked old." The guy was twenty-five years older than her. What was he thinking?

"Let's get out. I'll spring for a taxi," Ilana said as she rapped the rear windshield of the cab with her knuckles. "I think my obligation to Grandpops is over."

The men agreed to let us off at the next gas station. Ilana called a taxi and we waited in the crisp autumn night.

"You won't abandon me, will you," she said quietly.

"But we're both going home now."

She shook her head but I knew what she meant. After I had blown tonight's match so badly, *I* owed *her*. The taxi dropped me off at the Bernsteins' where I unlocked the keypad and tiptoed into the dark vestibule.

The hall flooded with light. "Rain?" It was Leah. "Where were you?"

My mind raced. How on earth was I going to get out of this one? "Rain, what's going on? It's almost *midnight*."

"I . . . I had to work on a project with someone in my class," I said as I brushed a clump of grass from my skirt. "It was a social . . . studies project."

She narrowed her eyes. "With who?"

"You don't know the name," I said as I edged past her and scurried upstairs to the safety of my bedroom.

chapter 14

>>——→ The Red Sox Are Home ←——≪

The next day I got back two failed quizzes: history and math. Matchmaven was definitely taking a toll on my life. After school I trudged into the kitchen where I found Bubby Bayla sitting at the table filling in a crossword puzzle. An envelope lay in front of her.

"This is yours, Rain," she said, sipping from a mug that reeked of coffee substitute.

I grabbed the envelope, and looked down at my dad's handwriting. The familiar scrawl was a flood of sunshine, coating me like caramel.

"Open it!" Bubby said.

This was one bored Bubby. "Can I have a second, please?"

I said. I wanted to savour the angular handwriting before I tore it open.

Inside was a framed photo of me and my dad at a ball game from two years ago, with a short note tucked into the back.

> *Dear Rainy,*
> *Since I can't be there to watch the games with you, I*
> *convinced Mira to upgrade her cable package to get all*
> *the MLB sports stations. You'll be able to watch the new*
> *Red Sox games in the spring as a reward for what I know*
> *is going to be a successful school year. In the meantime,*
> *you can catch some re-runs (after your homework and*
> *chores are done, of course) — there's a great Ortiz game*
> *this Sunday. Enjoy and have a great week.*
> *Love, Daddy*

"So?" Bubby asked.

Technically I've lived most of my life in New England. If we weren't living in Boston we spent a month every summer with my grandparents in Brookline, Massachusetts. We'd go to at least four ball games while we visited and more when we lived in Boston or Providence.

To me the Red Sox are home.

"My dad got me all the baseball channels," I said, turning to leave. "There's a classic David Ortiz game this Sunday."

"Big deal." Bubby snorted. "Players today are a bunch of overpaid children."

I scooped up the envelope, ready to flee.

"They don't make them like they used to," she said.

"With all due respect, Bubby," I said, "that cliché is *so* 1950. Ortiz is one of the most talented hitters in the league."

"With all due respect, young lady, if you never saw Ted Williams hit then you don't know from talent."

I paused.

"Believe you me, *that* was a player," she said, rapping her clenched knuckles on the kitchen table with surprising geriatric energy.

Bubby Bayla? The *Red Sox*? I turned back to the kitchen.

"You're kidding, right?"

"Your butterballs are like midgets. I saw the Red Sox play in Fenway Park back in 1948. Now *that* was a team. Mickey McDermott pitched and Williams played."

"Wow." I dropped into a kitchen chair. "Fenway Park? But are you . . . from Boston?"

"Please," she said. "Toronto. But back before the Blue Jays or the old Exhibition Stadium, I had the Sox."

"But what about Uncle Eli?"

Her eyes squeezed shut and she clutched her chest, like she had angina.

"Are you okay?" I said, alarmed.

"You're giving me a conniption," she said breathlessly. Which I found both confusing and disturbing. I mean can you actually *give* someone a conniption? Were they contagious?

Do conniptions even exist?

Fortunately she opened her eyes and calmly took a sip of non-coffee. I breathed a sigh of relief that the conniption was over.

The wall clock ticked in the silent kitchen as a plan hatched in my head. "You know, the game is supposed to be a pretty exciting one."

She shrugged.

I sighed and thought about my pathetically non-existent

social life. Tamara and Jeremy and Dahlia Engel aside, of course. And Professor K.

"Would you like to watch the game with me?" It was an olive branch. And a very generous one on my part. Maybe old people were the only friends I could make at this point. I mean I did like knishes and seltzer, after all.

Bubby eyed me with a mixture of surprise and suspicion. "Nah."

This was how low I'd sunk — I was being rejected by a cranky great-grandmother.

"But what if we got some snacks," I said, zeroing in on Bubby's weakness. "Maybe, you know, invite some other people. Who like the Red Sox."

Yes, I admit it. *I was groveling.*

"You'll get some nice food? Maybe even some chips?" Bubby said. I swear she was eighty going on six.

"For sure," I said. "It'll be like a party."

"Fine. Sunday night, when your aunt and uncle are at the wedding." I was disappointed about having to wait five days to watch the game together but I thought better of arguing with her in case she changed her mind. At least it gave me something to look forward to. And considering the state of my social affairs, it was a big deal.

Maybe I wasn't cut out to be a matchmaker, but I'd planned some choice parties last year with Maya and Danielle. I decided to turn the Red Sox "party" into a geriatric extravaganza. I drew up a red-food themed menu that was salt-free and low in cholesterol.

Over the next few days I bought red plastic-ware and cut out large socks from red construction paper. It was the only break that I took from matchmaking. Aunt Mira was pleased that I was taking the initiative in looking after Bubby so she generously threw in thirty dollars for refreshments. This was progress; it was a new peak on the Mira frontier.

Leah even smiled at me a few times. Suddenly I wasn't planning a party because I was lonely and bored. I was doing a good *deed*. For the *elderly*.

My mother called the next evening.

"Honey, I'm so proud of you. Aunt Mira told me that you're making a lovely party for her mother-in-law's friends." I sank into the couch in the family room. Bubby wasn't around, for a change.

"Actually," I said. "I'm kind of charged about it. We're going to watch a Red Sox game thanks to Daddy."

"I've never really thought of Mrs. Bernstein as a baseball fan, but go figure," Mom said.

"I guess Toronto is full of surprises."

"Rain, are things going okay?" she said, which meant that news of the two failed quizzes hadn't travelled across the ocean. "Are you meeting people?" Clearly she *had* been talking with Mira. I saw no reason why Professor K. or Bubby's friends didn't count. And the concern in my mother's voice wasn't hard to miss.

"Don't worry, Mom. I'm fine," I said, thinking of Dahlia. I guess you could say that one non-hostile conversation was the new companionship. And I now had Bubby's crew to party with.

After all, what are six or seven decades between friends?

chapter 15

>>—→ Five Full Days of Dread ←—«

I was a bit shaken up after Ilana and Jonathan's dating debacle. Introducing Tamara and Jeremy had been so easy; I had no idea that matchmaking could be so complicated.

I briefly considered ending my illustrious matchmaking career, after eight distinguished days of service. But there was no way I was going to abandon Ilana after that horror-show date. And Leah needed even more help. On Monday I entered the kitchen in pursuit of licorice and I found Mira buttoning up her blazer.

"Leah, please come," she said as she arranged her scarf. "Sheva Brand is such a fantastic speaker, I'm sure you'd enjoy her."

"Is it . . . women only?" Leah said.

"One hundred percent," Mira said with a knowing look. Leah was so terrified of running into Ben, she never left the house when she wasn't at work or at school.

Leah stood at the bay window at the back of the kitchen, her fingers on the glass as she stared out at the park. "I don't mind staying home, Aunt Mira," she said in a soft voice. "I can start to cook for Shabbos."

Which was *five* days away. Leah was a plant slowly dying of thirst.

"I'd love you to get out a bit," Mira said.

"I'm fine. Really. I'm excited to try a new apple crisp recipe that I found on the internet."

And no, she was not excited to try a new apple crisp recipe that she found on the internet.

Aunt Mira turned to me with a pleading look, but I was the last person that Leah would listen to right now. Leah was wasting away. More motivated than ever, I returned to my room and opened my Matchmaven email.

I simply *had* to find love for Leah.

Once again I threw schoolwork to the wind and ploughed through the emails again, more determined than ever. At 9 p.m. I finally settled on a date for Leah.

Daniel Sharfstein.

It's true that he was jittery but Leah was kind and would put him at ease. He was thirty — an appropriate age for her. He was a runner — like Leah. He adored kids. Leah would love that.

Matchmaven had no problem selling Daniel to her. She was eager to date and apparently nobody was fixing her up.

Daniel requested a Sunday night date, which happened to

coincide with Mira and Eli going out to the wedding as well as my fabulous Red Sox party. Everything had to be carefully choreographed after Leah took stock of my party decorations and begged Mira and Eli to make me wait until after Daniel had picked her up before setting up for the Red Sox party. No problem there. I wanted Leah to be as calm and positive as possible for her date with Daniel. And besides, Mira was insistent that I catch up on all of my homework before setting up for the party.

The date was less than a week away. So while I ran around buying red streamers and special snacks, Leah and Daniel were able to enjoy five full days of dread and self-doubt. I spent the better part of Tuesday night on Professor Kellman's computer instant messaging Daniel with details about the date. The more Daniel's composure deteriorated, the greater my sense of unease grew. He agonized over what to wear, where to take Leah, and what to talk about. One thing he knew for sure was that he was going to take more than one set of spare clothes to discreetly change into if the sweating got out of control.

What was I thinking?

Even Leah needed to be coaxed.

> **Leah:** I'm going to be honest, Maven. My confidence is pretty shaky now.
> **Matchmaven:** You're a beautiful, smart, and kind woman.
> **Leah:** I appreciate the compliment, but you don't really know that.

I do, Leah, I do.

> **Leah:** My life was so much simpler six months ago. I still can't believe that I'm dating again.

Matchmaven: Everything has a reason. I have no doubt that you'll have a fabulous new husband and you'll be relieved that you didn't marry your ex-fiancé.

Leah: I guess.

Matchmaven: I'm sure of it. You'll even thank your sister!

Leah: Whoa. I'm not there yet.

Okay, it might have been too soon. But I could see that Matchmaven had the potential to grow into a dual-purpose enterprise. Marry off Leah and get me back in her good books.

In the meantime Daniel was starting to freak me out. He absolutely could not go full-out nerd on this date.

Daniel: I'm just so awful on dates.

Matchmaven: Clearly.

Daniel: How am I going to calm myself down?

Matchmaven: What makes U relaxed?

Daniel: I don't know. Kids. My nieces and nephews. My dog.

Matchmaven: Well you're obviously not taking kids with you on a date.

I was ready to throw up.

Matchmaven: You MUST stay calm. Just do whatever it takes to stay calm. You have to stop acting like you haven't been on a date for five years.

Daniel: Actually, it's only been four and a half years.

Daniel: Maven?

Daniel: Maven? Are you there?

This was so outside of my skill set, I might as well have been repairing air conditioners. How did I come to advise grown men about their personal lives?

> **Matchmaven:** Just remember that Leah is naturally wonderful and kind. You'll be fine.
> **Daniel:** I appreciate it. I like natural! She's not into that heavy makeup and high heels, right?
> **Matchmaven:** She's totally natural.

At least she *was* totally natural — once upon a time.

On Sunday evening, the night of the date, I stared in abject horror as she descended the stairs with makeup caked on so thick that you'd need a salting truck to cut through it.

I gasped out loud. "I know, Rain," Aunt Mira said with an admiring smile. "Doesn't she look beautiful?"

No, she did *not* look beautiful. Leah looked like a freak show clown on three-inch stilts. She was so obviously lacking self-confidence, because she never *ever* would have packed on so much paint. I mean she's stunning, she doesn't need it.

I shot out of the kitchen into the main floor powder room and whipped out my cell phone to see if I could g-chat her. It was probably too late to intercept her before Daniel arrived but it was worth an attempt any way.

> Hi Leah,
> I just wanted to wish you luck on your date with Daniel.
> He's probably going to take you to a coffee shop so
> nice-casual dress will be awesome, no heels or anything.

Daniel's a real earthy guy so I'm sure you'll be beautiful.

Hugs,

Matchmaven

What was I thinking? Daniel would be here any minute. I bounded back into the kitchen, where Mira, all dressed up for the wedding, was applying a coat of lipstick. Plan B was formulating in my mind.

Since Daniel hadn't arrived I had a tiny window to salvage the situation.

Aunt Mira and Uncle Eli were still admiring the post-Expressionist oil painting that was my sister's face when I re-entered the kitchen.

"Leah, you look so pretty," I said. She nodded while smoothing down the folds of her pleated skirt.

Since I didn't exactly have time on my hands, I jumped right in. "Are you sure you need that much blush and eye shadow, though?"

"Rain!" Mira said as Leah's hands flew up to her cheeks.

"It's just that she's naturally beautiful," I said. "She doesn't need to cover up her skin so much."

Mira's nostrils flared as she threw a warning look at me.

"Is it my clothes too?" Leah said in horror looking down at her outfit. "I haven't shopped since I was in New York. I have nothing to wear."

"Your outfit is beautiful," Aunt Mira said to Leah as she glared at me.

"But this is my only outfit," Leah moaned.

"When the two of you go down to New York for the Saunders bar mitzvah in January, you can do a little shopping," Mira said. "In the meantime you look stunning."

"But maybe she doesn't need to be so formal. Like with those heels," I said looking at her feet. "I mean if they're only going to a coffee shop."

Leah's eyes popped open. "How did you know —?"

I shuffled back a step. Leah didn't know that Rain knew that Matchmaven had arranged a coffee shop date. "It's just a usual place for a first date," I blurted. "Isn't it?"

"I have to change," Leah gasped as she fled the kitchen toward the staircase.

"Rain!" Mira clamped my arm. "Did you know that this is Leah's first date since the engagement?"

I gulped and shook my head.

"We need to build her up, not tear her down."

I nodded obediently with a sorrowful look. But my work was done.

Leah finally re-emerged in the kitchen and sure enough she had enough makeup removed that you could actually see the contour of her face. She was also wearing flats now.

"Leah, you look beautiful," I said.

"That's what you said last time," she said.

"I was being nice," I said. "Now I'm being honest." See? I can do both.

She squinted her eyes. "Have you been reading my emails or something?"

"Wh . . . what?"

"The matchmaker told me the same thing."

"Please," I said. "It's just common sense."

Mira shook her head as Uncle Eli chuckled.

When the doorbell rang, Uncle Eli straightened his tie and headed to the front door. Aunt Mira tucked in her blouse and trailed him to the entrance to welcome Daniel. What can

I say — that's the way it works with us. The five-minute reconnaissance mission with the boy. No last-minute psychopaths on our watch.

"You can go upstairs," Leah muttered, which was patently unfair since I had made the match and I at least deserved to see what Daniel looked like. But I wasn't exactly in a bargaining position.

I stood on the top of the stairs straining to pick up any snippet of conversation, but I couldn't see or hear much of anything. Daniel was either super-quiet or super-nervous. Or both.

Mira and Eli left for the wedding right after Daniel picked up Leah. I was finally free to set up the party so I rushed to the kitchen and pulled the fruit and vegetables out of the fridge and began arranging them on a silver tray from Mira's china hutch. I poured a mound of Grape-Nuts in a bowl then piled a heap of salt-free chips on a platter. Thanks to my careful planning, Bubby and her friends would be able to savour a safe and healthy menu while enjoying the game.

Bubby was visiting with her best friend Mrs. Feldman, the one she was always fighting with, and they were scheduled to return by 7:30 to help put the finishing touches on the party.

With the prune juice and seltzer chilling in the fridge, I unwrapped the evening's prized delicacy, a rare gift pried from the reluctant butcher at the kosher supermarket: three pounds of authentic *kishka*, beef intestines that were popular with my grandparents' generation but hardly anybody ate anymore. This was the real thing, with the real stuffing.

Apparently it's illegal for hygiene reasons.

I zapped the *kishka* and held my breath as an unusual stench wafted from the microwave. It looked gorgeous in a gleaming ceramic bowl that Aunt Mira used for entertaining. I artfully garnished it with two sprigs of cilantro. It looked like the kind of gourmet intestines you'd find in a trendy cooking magazine. When it was all set up, I admired my spread on the coffee table. It looked attractive but something was missing: greenery.

I peered out the window of the den at the cedar and pine trees in the park. With only thirty minutes left until the party, there was no time to grab a pair of gardening shears. I'd never really paid any attention to Mira's plants but I scoured the living room with a new pair of eyes. A large dieffenbachia plant sat in the corner of the living room but its leaves were too gigantic for the party platters.

Six tiny plants sat on a tapestry runner on Mira's antique sideboard. Although my mother was an indoor gardener, I wasn't familiar with these miniature plants. They almost looked like trees. They'd have to do. I grabbed a pair of scissors from the kitchen, cut off a pile of the petite branches, and filled a plastic baggie full of leaves. The little trees looked kind of bare when I'd finished but I figured they would grow back their branches in no time.

I meticulously placed the miniscule branches and foliage around the platters of food on the coffee table. The presentation looked fabulous.

The doorbell rang and I strode to the entrance to let in Bubby Bayla. But when I pulled back the door, I was surprised to see Dahlia standing on the porch. She waved a flash drive in front of me. "Hi," she said. "I've got the spreadsheet set up."

I blinked.

"Remember I offered? I know the whole thing is a secret so I figured you wouldn't want to do it at school. Right?"

"I really appreciate this," I said. "But I'm kind of in the middle of something now."

Her face fell. "I should have checked first."

"I'm kind of throwing a party."

"Well, I wouldn't want to disturb you and your friends," she said as she dropped the flash drive into her pocket. She turned to leave when a shiny Ford Mustang, as red as a fire engine, screeched into the driveway. The front doors of the car burst open and an elderly woman climbed out from the driver's side while Bubby Bayla clambered onto the driveway.

"Raina!" the driver said as she waved her cane at me.

"Hi," I said. "Are you Mrs. Feldman?"

"I am," she said as she slowly climbed out of the car and hobbled up the driveway. She wore a baggy trench coat that matched the shade of her hair and the colour of her face; she was essentially five feet of grey. Or maybe more like four feet. Mrs. Feldman clutched the railing to haul herself up the stairs.

"Can I help you?" Dahlia said to her, turning down the stairs.

Mrs. Feldman fended Dahlia off with her cane. "What? You think I'm some kind of invalid?"

"Sylvia, she's just trying to help," Bubby said as she followed Mrs. Feldman up the concrete stairs. She cast a glance at Dahlia. "You here for the party too? What's your name?"

"Dahlia."

"We have lots of room," Mrs. Feldman said, wheezing, as she summited the porch. "Irving Goldblatt's bursitis flared up." She clipped her cane on the concrete and limped past Dahlia.

"Lillian Shimmel isn't coming either," Mrs. Feldman added. "She has the runs again, the poor thing."

Dahlia froze.

"What, you need a personal invitation to come in the house?" Bubby said to Dahlia as she lumbered past her. "Don't be such a prima donna."

Dahlia threw me a questioning look and I shrugged in response. You really didn't want to say no to Bubby. We piled into the front hall and Dahlia stared in wonderment at the riot of red; there were streamers, posters, and balloons festooning the walls. "What is this?" Dahlia said.

"It's a Red Sox party."

The doorbell rang. "Hang on a second," I said as an ancient woman with sweeping blue bangs stepped inside the house. I was delighted because my parents used to reminisce about older women dying their hair pale blue when they were kids. I had never been able to picture what it looked like until now. If I had more foresight I would have worn a blue solidarity wig for my new friends.

"It's a party for all my friends in Toronto," I said to Dahlia as I pointed to the two women shuffling toward the den.

"I'm Dorothy," the woman said to Dahlia. "What's your name?"

"Um, Dahlia."

"And you're Raina," Dorothy said with a warm smile. The doorbell rang again and an elderly gentleman with a polished scalp hobbled into the foyer, leaning on a lacquered cane.

"Dolinsky, here," he said, all business.

"Hi, Dolinsky," I said. "Party's in the back."

"I brought some compote," Dorothy said, raising a beige plastic container. "Dahlia, can you take it to the kitchen?"

"Yeah. Sure," she said.

"Raina, we saved a space for your friend," Mrs. Feldman shouted from the family room.

Dahlia shot me a gaze, her brows furrowed with confusion.

"Why don't you just hang out for the first inning and then you can make your getaway," I murmured. Dahlia nodded in response.

Dorothy handed the container to Dahlia then threaded her hand through Dahlia's arm and they shuffled to the back of the house.

With only a tiny interlude available, I stepped into the powder room and fished out my cell phone. It was unlikely that I'd hear from Leah during the date, but I had to be on call just in case there was a problem. Especially after the Ilana/Jonathan fiasco.

Since there was no news, I dropped the phone into my skirt pocket and wandered to the den. There were now six seniors lounging on the furniture, with Dahlia wedged between Dorothy and Mrs. Feldman on the leather couch. She shot me a pleading look.

"You didn't come to take your friend away, did you?" Dorothy said, gently pinching Dahlia's cheek as her face contorted in misery. "It's so lovely when young people visit."

I shrugged apologetically to Dahlia. "Everybody ready?" I scooped up the remote and clicked the power button on the huge flat screen television.

"The Sox have always had such wonderful players," Dorothy said. I gazed at the tiny Red Sox aficionado sitting on the leather couch and felt my heart swelling.

"Bob Gillespie," Dolinsky said. "Him, I'm really looking forward to watching."

"On the Sox roster?"

"Of course," he said with a snort. "The Red Sox."

"Oh," I said, annoyed that I hadn't been able to keep up with recent trades.

"And Charlie Maxwell too." An elderly man wearing a jacket and cravat wheezed.

Who?

"Lou Stringer," Mrs. Feldman said. "Now there's an infielder."

The reality of my exile swallowed me like a carwash. I couldn't believe that my father hadn't bothered to mention this amount of trading in the last few weeks. I decided to let it go because the topic of this conversation was *fantastic*. The tiny men and women in this room spoke my language. They were my people.

"Well, to me no one will ever come close to Ted Williams," Bubby said.

It was Mozart.

"Please everyone, help yourself to some refreshments," I announced. I hit the button on the cable remote and flopped on the floor in front of the TV.

The familiar voices of Don Orsillo, the play-by-play announcer, and Jerry Remy wrapped me like a warm July day in Fenway Park. It felt like my father and grandfather were sitting on either side of me. The phantom scent of hot dogs teased my nostrils and crowded out the *kishka* and prunes that filled the air.

"I'm looking forward to seeing Dom DiMaggio play again," Mrs. Feldman said.

Wait a minute.

DiMaggio was born in 1917. In fact, I was absolutely certain that he retired in 1953.

"What is this?" Mrs. Feldman said, gesturing to the television. "Who are these people?"

"These are just the *new* players," Dolinsky said with disdain. I got it. This game was fifty years too recent for Bubby's friends. My heart sank as I watched the group rapidly lose interest. Within seconds it became almost impossible to hear the TV as Bubby's friends chattered above the play-by-play.

I picked up a plate and carried it to Dorothy. She was intently following an argument between Bubby and Mrs. Feldman.

"Sylvia, I'm telling you. Ida had *phlebitis*," Bubby was saying.

"Bayla?" Mrs. Feldman said in a rising voice. She was squeezing Dahlia's hand like she could empty out the air in Bubby's argument. "If I've told you once, I've told you a thousand times. *It was a goiter.*"

The conversation was getting too controversial so I scooped up the remote and raised the volume, but they just yelled even louder.

I rose to my feet, but no one noticed that I was completely blocking the television. Dahlia's eye followed my movement; she clearly smelled escape. "I'll be right back," she murmured to Mrs. Feldman.

Dahlia followed me to the kitchen, where my buffet adorned the island. *"What was that?"*

"That was a party," I said. "These . . . are . . . my Toronto friends."

She frowned.

"I mean except for Irving," I said about the no-show.

"Bursitis is such a drag," she said.

"And Lillian."

"Don't." Dahlia shook her head but she was smiling. "You can't discuss Lillian Shimmel . . . in the kitchen."

"Hey," I said. "You want a snack?"

She surveyed the buffet set out on the island and wrinkled her nose. "Don't take this personally. But no thanks."

"Yeah, it's gross. How about some real food?" I said as I pulled back the pantry door and pawed the junk shelf. "How about you and I break blondies."

"Underbaked?"

"Hmm . . . good point. Uh . . . how about red licorice?"

"Now you're talking." Dahlia snatched the giant bag from my hands and tried to pull open the plastic. She caught me watching her, and looked back, eyes narrowed. "What?"

"Nothing," I said. "Just . . . well . . . you said something earlier about a spreadsheet?"

She smiled. We left the party behind and climbed the stairs armed with a cell phone, a laptop, and a big bag of licorice.

And that's how I became friends with the girl who tested positive for Nerd.

chapter 16
→→→ ·A Tube of Heart Failure ←←←

Dahlia and I plopped onto my bed. She pulled her laptop from her knapsack and plugged in a pink flash drive.

I glanced at my phone, relieved to see that Leah hadn't contacted me. I ripped open the licorice and grabbed a string, then passed the bag to her.

"Here, check on my computer," Dahlia said, handing it over to me.

There were three emails from new clients, and two of them were from guys. I was going to have to be much more careful about fixing up Ilana than I had been the first time. What was with all these quirks? Matchmaven was like a matchmaking superhero to people with eccentric habits and issues. Which I guess was the whole point of Matchmaven.

"This is serious stuff," she said over my shoulder.

I started reading all of the emails I had received with a much more critical eye.

I couldn't take any chances with Ilana. I also had to allow for the super-slight possibility that Daniel and Leah wouldn't click, which would mean finding another guy for her. It truly was a numbers game. The larger the database, the more options I had.

"Okay," Dahlia said. "I think that one of us should read each email and then the other one inputs the information into the correct categories."

I bit into the licorice and pulled it. "You realize I have over forty names right now."

"That's okay," she said. "Our motto is No Single Left Behind."

"It's really not."

She stopped. "Then what's the point?"

I swallowed the licorice and sighed. "I'm trying to find a match for my sister but she doesn't know I'm Matchmaven."

Dahlia's eyes popped open. "Get out."

"It's a long and crazy story," I said. "Let's just say that I need to repair some really stupid stuff I've done."

"Do tell," she said knotting a piece of licorice and popping it into her mouth. "Is that why you had to move here?"

"Without getting into details, let's just say that I'm not quite as perfect as I appear."

She chuckled. I picked up my phone, slid the computer over to Dahlia, and began reading emails to her while she typed information into columns.

Thirty minutes later we were still entering the data, with both of us supplying running commentary on each person's matchability. The noise from downstairs steadily grew louder.

"I think they're really having fun," I said.

"For sure," Dahlia said. "They still have so many diseases to debate."

Twenty minutes later we finally finished setting up the spreadsheet.

"See how fantastic this is?" she said. "You have your categories for gender, age, and preferences, and then you can just click on any of the attributes if you're looking for something specific."

You had to love her. Dahlia had the soul of techie, trapped inside the body of a . . . techie. I definitely saw a makeover in her future.

"Okay, help me find someone for Ilana," I said. We surveyed the list, struggling with every option. Each time I thought I'd chosen someone for Ilana, Dahlia changed my mind with a counterargument.

We finally narrowed the list to three men: Aaron, Mark, and Reuben. Mark seemed like the most mainstream person in the whole database. Aaron, the scary-smart mathematics doctoral student who turned into a blubbering child around women emerged as another possibility. Dahlia liked Reuben, the pediatric surgeon who laughed inappropriately but I ruled him out. What if she thought that he was laughing at *her*? It was unlikely but I was terrified of insulting her after the last date. Was I being too picky about this? I mean, on paper they all appeared like they could have been decent matches.

"How on earth do you do this?" Dahlia said as she flopped back on the bed. "This matchmaking is more complicated than a logarithm!"

"I know. It's almost a Nobel Prize category waiting to happen."

"I think I'll just provide the tech support from now on. And of course, I can lend a helping hand with the junk food."

"Speaking of which, it's time to replenish," I said, glancing at my watch. I noted with surprise that it was 9:30 already. "It's *really* loud down there," I said.

"Well, they can't hear each other," she said.

"We better check it out."

Things became clear when we reached the foot of the stairs.

Twenty-five additional seniors were milling around the living room and dining room. Now I understood why Bubby wanted to have the party on a night when Mira and Eli were at a wedding. And bonus points for Leah being out of the house too. Everywhere I looked, Bubby's elderly friends wielded plates of salted pretzels and chips, like bite-sized grenades. I raced into the kitchen. Unfamiliar snacks covered the kitchen table: salty crackers, packaged cookies, and Pringles potato chips. Two glass salad bowls brimmed with green olives and pickles.

The sodium was flowing like water from a tap. Dahlia and I both gaped at the scene in the kitchen. Cholesterol-raising foods were everywhere. A crystal bowl sat defiantly on the counter holding the remnants of a creamy chocolate mousse that looked like it had been decorated with a tube of heart failure. With shaking hands, I whipped out my cell phone and quickly programmed 911 on speed dial. I couldn't afford to lose any time when the first heart attack occurred.

Bad seniors. I anxiously scoured the front hall, fearful

that Mira and Eli might walk in any minute. I needed to find Bubby — now.

I charged into the family room where I found her seated on the leather couch holding court over Mrs. Feldman, Dorothy, and four other women I didn't recognize.

"Um, Bubby? There are a lot of snacks here that might not be so, you know, healthy for your friends?" My voice was cracking. "Do you know where they came from?"

"Raina," she said, hauling herself off the sofa. "Come with me."

I trailed behind her as she lumbered to the dining room. She lowered her voice. "While you and your friend were hiding upstairs, Mrs. Feldman drove me to Sobeys to get something edible." She pointed at the bowl of Grape-Nuts on the counter. "What's with all the hospital food?"

With Bubby's appetite for junk food, that credit card of hers was like a lethal weapon. She turned and hobbled back to the den where her friends awaited her return and she could channel her inner Shira Wasser.

I stomped to the kitchen table where Dahlia was busy grabbing a foil pan filled with cold, congealed pigs in blankets and emptying it into the compost bin. Even after we threw out all the offending food, then what? I wasn't exactly going to start wrestling s'mores out of tiny, bony hands.

I dumped a bowl of cheese curls in the garbage then I turned around and gasped.

Mira and Leah both stood behind me. I reeled back.

"What exactly is going on here?" Mira bellowed, flames shooting out of her nostrils. Well, it seemed that way, anyway.

Leah's mouth hung open in shock.

One of Mira's hands held a beaded clutch while her other

one grasped the counter. Her furious eyes bore into mine.

"I didn't do this . . ." I faltered.

"This just appeared?" Mira waved at the spread on the counter.

"No, someone brought it when I went upstairs."

"Upstairs," Leah said.

"I don't recall you hosting a party *upstairs*," Mira said, her eyes two brown bombs of rage. My heart pounded. Dahlia shrunk back away from the kitchen.

"Just for a bit —"

Leah's hand flew to her chest and she turned to Mira. "I shouldn't have gone out tonight," she said. "I'm so sorry Aunt Mira. I should have made sure to be here to supervise Rain." I couldn't help it. I studied her face for a split second, looking for physical tells. Good date or bad date?

"It's not your fault, Leah," Eli said in a soothing voice.

Mira glared at the scene around her and stamped into the den.

"You need to see the spread I put out," I said to Eli and Leah, pleading. "I bought healthy foods. I didn't bring any of this into the house." Eli shrugged with a sympathetic smile.

Mira stomped back to the kitchen, and stood in front of me, her eyes watery now.

"My bonsai trees . . ." Her hand flew to her forehead and she closed her eyes. "What did you do to my bonsais?" Her voice was shaking. It was actually kind of scary.

"Oh, no," Leah said, a look of horror spreading across her face.

"What are bonsais?" I said to Eli in a hoarse whisper.

"They're miniature trees," Eli said in a gentle voice.

"They take years to cultivate," Leah said in a whisper. "What were you thinking?"

"Those little plants?" I said, my lips trembling. "I clipped a couple of leaves to decorate my spread."

Bubby was rapidly shooing her friends out of the house.

"I can't do this, Eli," Mira said. "She's a bad influence on Bubby."

I was a bad influence on Bubby? If anything, *Bubby* was a bad influence on *me*.

"I'll clean up with Rain and Leah," Eli said in a quiet voice to Mira. "You help these people get home."

Mira-Zombie obediently turned and shuffled to the living room.

"Mr. Bernstein, I can take some of these guests home too," Dahlia said.

"Thank you." Uncle Eli nodded. "And you're who?"

"Dahlia Engel."

"Nice to meet you Dahlia," Uncle Eli said. "That would be helpful."

Dahlia followed Mira into the family room.

"Rain, come with me," Uncle Eli said. Leah tipped a bowl of potato chips into the green compost bin. I felt myself choking with dread as Eli led me to his office.

He ushered me inside and motioned for me to sit on the opposite side of his heavy antique desk.

"So you bought all that juice, Grape-Nuts, and the other stuff?" he said.

I nodded, too terrified to speak.

"The prunes too?"

"Pitted," I whispered. Which cost me around three dollars more for the bag, not that I was going to get a pat on the back for that right now.

He sighed slowly with a faint smile.

"Rain. I probably shouldn't tell you this." He hesitated for a moment. "My mother is a very special woman who managed to hold my family together when my father died. Thank god, her strength is a gift. But it's difficult for her to live without independence now that she's here with Mira and me."

He shook his head. "She lived in a retirement residence for a while. But there were . . . how should I put it . . . *incidents*."

"Incidents?" I said in a squeaky voice.

"Yes. She was 'counselled' out of Shalom Gardens," he said. I blinked.

"Rain, I'll be frank. She was asked to leave."

It's not like Eli needed to explain to me what getting counselled out of an institution meant.

"She was constantly ordering in fast food," Eli said. "Onion rings, pizza, french fries, you name it. She also managed to get a steady supply of tequila and limes. Even after we took away her blender, half her floor was begging their families to bring them margaritas. It was no use removing her credit card. She's an extraordinarily . . . *resourceful* woman."

Eli leaned back in his chair and sighed. "The management of the facility felt that her behaviour posed a risk to herself and the other residents."

No surprise there.

"Look, Mira loves you. She's trying to help you and your mother out. I know you wanted to stay in New York and I'm sorry it didn't work out with Aunt Naomi. But I want you to know that I think you're a fine young lady and I believe you'll succeed. I'll try talking to Aunt Mira."

"Thank you," I said, my voice quivering.

"Now let's go help Leah with the mess," he said, rising from his chair. I stood up and just as I turned the knob he spoke.

"By the way, what was in that bowl? Was that actually real *kishka*?"

I nodded.

He smiled. "If it's alright with you, I think I'll have some for dinner tomorrow night."

"Okay," I said in a tiny voice.

We returned to the kitchen and the three of us filled two recycle bins with plastic plates, forks, and empty food packaging. I removed the streamers and decorations from the walls of the family room and returned the chairs to the dining room while Leah swept the wooden floors. It must have taken a while for Mira and Dahlia to wrangle and drive home Bubby's guests, because we heard our aunt's car pulling up in the driveway just as we finished putting the last bags in the garage.

"You can call it a night, Rain," Eli said, his eyes darting to the front door. I scooted upstairs, and almost made it to my bedroom when I heard Mira's voice.

"Raina."

Mira stood at the foot of the stairs.

"I'm so sorry about all of this, Aunt Mira," I said looking down. "I just —"

"I'm very disappointed with what happened tonight," she said, her voice tight. "It was completely irresponsible to disappear from your own party."

"I'm so sorry, Aunt Mira."

"I'm *trusting* you to turn a new leaf here." She gazed at me with a pained expression. "Your mother would not be happy with how tonight turned out."

"I'm sorry," I said in a squeak.

She shook her head and stamped down to the kitchen.

chapter 17
Bronx

The next morning I got an email from Daniel.

Leah's fantastic. Will contact you later.

I didn't have a chance to enjoy that email because there was a more worrisome one from Leah. She urgently begged me for my phone number, promising that she wouldn't share it or ask my name.

Since I obviously couldn't give her my number I'd have to wait for her to email details. And I waited all day.

That evening, Eli drove Mira, Leah, Bubby, and me to Tamara and Jeremy's engagement party. When we arrived at the catering hall, Mira held me back while the others entered the building.

"Mrs. Levine isn't happy with your performance at school."

"I just need some time," I said with a pleading look. Matchmaven had overtaken my life.

"I don't want any more complaints from her," Mira said with a stern nod.

We finally entered the facility and I was caught off guard by the size of the crowd. You wouldn't have known that Tamara and Jeremy were both from out of town by the number of people there. There were easily 150 guests, which even included a number of familiar faces from Moriah. The rabbi from the Bernsteins' *shul* was in attendance, apparently with half of his membership too. Both Jeremy's parents and Tamara's had flown in for the occasion along with Jeremy's two older sisters.

A line of buffet tables laden with petit fours, cream-filled cakes, and martini glasses filled with berries bisected the dance floor. The air was so thick with the scents of Givenchy, Chanel, and Hermès that your dress could get wet. I observed Tamara and Jeremy across a lake of pastries. Her entire face was lit up in a smile as she and Jeremy stood at the centre of a throng of well-wishers. Her red hair was tied back in a loose updo. The beige chiffon folds of her gown wrapped softly around her. It was still early in the evening, so the keyboard music hadn't yet been cranked up to the deafening levels that would make virtually all conversation impossible.

Not that I had anyone to talk to. I glanced at my watch. Where was Professor K. already, my seventy-five-year-old bro? Bubby and Mrs. Feldman were stationed in chairs on the opposite side of the room from the dessert table, and I made a mental note to steer clear. Since the Party Gone Bad, I needed to avoid Bubby like hydrogenated oil. Or at least the way I should have avoided it. It wasn't that I was angry at her. I even admired her a bit after Eli's talk. But I definitely had to watch out for her. She was one naughty Bubby.

I loaded up my plate with rum balls and bit into the perfect brownie, so under-baked it was really just glorified goo. Tamara waved her arms at me to join her and Jeremy. I weaved my way through the crowd and gave Tamara a furtive hug, glancing behind my shoulder to make sure that Leah didn't see me acting too happy.

"Congratulations, guys," I said. "*Mazel tov.*"

"You're the hero today," Jeremy said, turning to me. "I wish we could thank you publicly, but don't worry."

Tamara leaned into me. "I'm actually being sent to Vancouver again for my work."

My face fell. "Nooo! How will I survive the Number 7 without you?"

"I'll be there for six weeks," she said shaking her head. "What can I do?"

"When will you see Jeremy?"

"We'll take turns flying out to visit each other," she said. "Planning the wedding will be a challenge though."

"Let me know if I can help," I said.

"You have already," she said with a warm smile. "More than you can imagine."

I wandered the hall observing everyone else having someone to talk to when I felt a tap on my shoulder.

"Hey!" Dahlia said.

"Hey, you," I said. "I didn't know you were coming!"

"I'm not really here," she said. "Jeremy does work for my dad. I just drove my parents here. I only popped in to see what your couple looks like."

"Oh," I said, disappointed. Dahlia shrugged and pointed at

my plate with the remnants of the brownies.

"They're perfect," I said.

"I know. Perfectly congealed cake batter."

A familiar voice rang out from behind me.

"Rain! *Mazel tov!* I've been thinking about you." The smile fled from Dahlia's face and she promptly melted into the crowd. I spun around. It was Mrs. Marmor.

This is one of the many joys of being in a tight community. You're all glammed up for an elegant engagement party and you turn around and the freaking *shrink* is standing next to you eating a cocktail wiener.

I seriously needed to lose Mrs. Marmor so I pretended to receive a phone call.

"I'm really sorry, Mrs. Marmor," I said. "Can you give me a minute? I'm expecting a *very* important phone call." From one of the legions of friends that I *don't* have, of course.

"I just want to speak to you for one minute," Mrs. Marmor said.

I flipped open my phone and took a quick look at my emails.

There was an email from Leah. I brought the phone to my ear.

"How *are* you?" I said in an exaggerated tone. I pointed to the phone and held up my index finger to Mrs. Marmor. *I'm busy, lady. Go get an éclair.* I nodded vigorously into the phone until Mrs. Marmor gave up and wandered over to the Sweet table.

I'd barely been in this town for two months and I was bumping into practically everyone I knew. Welcome to the Jewish community where there's only 1.1 degrees of separation. Like, who was going to show up next? Mrs. Levine?

Well, colour me a sorceress. Mrs. Levine entered the banquet hall a minute later.

This was supposed to be an engagement party. An engagement that happened because of me, I must say. But it felt more like being trapped inside some nightmarish video game, where school officials try to catch you and ruin your life. I ducked, dodged, and rotated, finally fleeing to the lobby.

Peering at my phone, I noticed that Leah had just emailed me.

> **Matchmaven:** Soooooo???
> **Leah:** It was . . . interesting.

I glanced over my shoulder and noted that Mrs. Levine was heading in my direction. She wore a royal blue suit sewn, once again, entirely from man-made fibres — the kind of fabric that comes out of the washing machine completely dry. Like a tablecloth.

I crossed the lobby and scuttled down the stairs to safety. I wasn't taking any chances. If Mrs. Levine saw me at a party she might have to think up some new restrictions.

> **Leah:** He seemed friendly when he picked me up. He's actually kind of cute. Right away it felt nice.
> **Matchmaven:** Awesome!!!!!

My matchmaking skills were definitely improving. I was parked at the bottom of the stairs in the dark hallway. A caretaker wielding a bucket and mop sailed past me. I scanned the doors, looking for an empty room to continue this conversation. Daniel thought she was great. She thought he was cute. I was liking where this was going.

> **Leah:** So he tells me that we're going for coffee and then
> we'll take a walk.
>
> **Matchmaven:** Sounds good.

I drifted down the hall toward a sign indicating the women's bathroom. I needed a solitary place to savour this conversation.

> **Leah:** So I get in the car and all of a sudden this thing
> jumps up out of nowhere and it's slimy, with hot air com-
> ing out of it. It blinds me and I start screaming.

I stopped. What?

> **Leah:** But I couldn't actually scream because a million tiny
> hairs fill my mouth. I couldn't even breathe.
>
> **Matchmaven:** What??????
>
> **Leah:** Daniel was so apologetic, but it was terrifying.

"Terrifying," I said out loud to myself. This conversation was like a foreign movie with no subtitles.

> **Leah:** He explained that it was just Bronx.
>
> **Matchmaven:** Bronx?

Couldn't she just come out and say what happened?

> **Leah:** His dog.
>
> **Matchmaven:** He brought his DOG on a DATE?
>
> **Leah:** Because of you.
>
> **Matchmaven:** Is he crazy?

Leah: He said you told him to bring the dog because he
gets nervous.

"I never told him to take his dog on the date," I said out
loud to myself.

I must have been yelling because the caretaker poked his
head out of the utility closet. I pushed open the door to the
women's bathroom and slipped inside.

The pink-tiled bathroom had two stalls and I stepped into
the unoccupied one. If this was a battle for air in here, I'd say
that the air freshener was definitely taking down the oxygen. I
gasped for breath as I locked the door and lowered myself onto
the closed toilet seat.

Leah: I have to tell you. Despite what Daniel claims, I'm
not even sure that it's really a dog. It might actually be an
antelope.

I remembered now. It was a Great Dane.

Leah: Well, anyway, Maven. The dog kept slobbering on
me. I spent the whole time in the car dodging the flight
path of his gob but he got my blouse.

I could feel my teeth grinding together. Please let this not
be another disastrous date.

Leah: Anyway, they wouldn't let Bronx into the coffee
shop and he seemed really upset.
Matchmaven: Why would Daniel be upset? You obviously
can't take a dog into a coffee shop.

Leah: No, I mean Bronx was really upset. LOL.

I giggled, and my laughter pinged across the bathroom.

Leah: So we took him to the park and threw balls.

Matchmaven: I really hope you're not mad at me.

Leah: No! It was actually funny. Daniel's sweet. I like him.

Matchmaven: Really?

I heaved a sigh of relief. I may have underestimated the place the dog occupied in Daniel's heart, but there seemed to be room for some connection with Leah in there too. She was always such a sport — I missed her so much. But if Rain couldn't have her, at least Matchmaven could for a bit.

A clatter shattered the quiet of the bathroom and echoed against the polished tiles. A round plastic blush compact tumbled to the floor from the next stall and landed inches from my shoe. There was a pause while I waited for a response from Leah.

Matchmaven: You still there?

Leah: Whoops, I just dropped my blush.

I lost my breath.

Leah: I'm hiding in the bathroom at an engagement party.

Before I could respond to her text, I looked down with horror as a hand that looked a lot like mine reached out and snatched the compact from the next stall.

My heart skipped a beat. *Leah was in the next stall.*

I had to get out of this bathroom now. Maybe if I flushed the toilet, I could open the door and make a run for it in less than five seconds.

I flushed. I opened the door a crack.

Leah stood in front of the sink tapping into her cell phone.

I slammed the stall door shut, panting. I was trapped. I glanced down at the phone. Thank goodness it was on silent.

> **Leah:** I so appreciate you helping me.

I steadied my breath, despite the air "freshener" so I could finish this conversation and get out.

> **Matchmaven:** So you want to see him again?
> **Leah:** LOL.
> **Matchmaven:** Does that mean yes?
> **Leah:** I could deal with a man with a dog, but I'm afraid what we have here is a bison with a man. Daniel was nice but it was just too weird. Please keep looking for me?
> **Matchmaven:** For sure.

I settled on the toilet and waited. I checked my phone and five minutes later it still didn't sound like the door to the bathroom had opened.

Soft sobs soon filled the bathroom. Leah was obviously not going anywhere.

"Mom?" She was talking to my mom now? "I'm so depressed," she said, weeping into her phone.

"I can't stand these engagement parties, especially because I really did have my eye on Jeremy. The dating scene is awful in Toronto. I hate that I'm only here because I was going to marry a Torontonian and now I'm so stuck here and lonely."

They chatted for half an hour while I shifted on the toilet seat, my bum increasingly prickling with pins and needles that radiated down my leg. If she didn't wrap it up, my entire lower body was going to lose all circulation and I'd have to be dragged out by my arms.

"And Rain is so irresponsible," she was saying now.

I held my breath. I couldn't stand to hear what was coming but I had nowhere to escape. "She's acting really weird — I don't know what's up with her. She just disappeared one evening last week and then snuck into the house at midnight. Honestly, she's so immature."

My eyes stung as she went on about me. *To my own mother.* She threw in a blow-by-blow description of Bubby's party gone bad, just in case Mira hadn't sufficiently alarmed my mother.

"I'm still upset with her about Ben," Leah said.

She listened while my mother said something to her.

"I know he was having doubts, Mom, but I think the idea that she wasn't being shipped back to live with you guys after she got kicked out of her school really bothered him. And having her move to Toronto was just the final straw. Like we were newlyweds that were going to have to babysit her."

She sighed. "I have no friends here and there's hardly anyone to go out with."

I buried my head in hands, just hoping this phone call would finally end.

"Thank goodness I found Matchmaven," she was saying. "I mean I just had this bizarre date with this monster-dog but the matchmaker is so sweet. I really like her. I wonder if she's my age. She's just got a young sensibility, very funny. I'm so lonely, Mom. I've never felt so low in my life. I feel so hopeless."

She finally ended her rant; I heard the water running and then she left the bathroom.

After a few minutes the coast was finally clear. I reached out and leaned over to unlock the door of the tiny stall, then rose from the toilet but all the circulation had drained from my feet and they had become rubber tubes. I collapsed on the floor with a loud crash.

The outer door to the bathroom burst open and Leah flew in. "Is everything okay —?"

Her eyes narrowed when she saw me. "Rain?" She bent over and pulled me to my feet. "What are you doing in here?"

I grabbed her arms and attempted to balance on my wobbly legs like a newborn foal. I clutched the sink and leaned in on my arms.

"My stomach was upset," I said. "I think it was the underbaked brownies. You should never eat that stuff. It's really not safe."

"How long were you in the bathroom?" She took a step back and studied my face. "Were you *following* me?"

"No! Of course not!"

She shook her head. "I don't know what's going on with you, but you've been acting very strange lately."

She turned and marched up the staircase back to the catering hall before I could say a word. I stood there, alone and deflated. Because apparently the more she liked Matchmaven, the less she cared for me.

chapter 18

≫———→ I'm Such an Idiot ←———≪

When I got home from school the next day, Mira was cooking canned salmon with boiled potatoes, which is unfortunate
because, in my opinion, there's no justification for any food
to ever be boiled.

I had received three new emails during the day, so I had a
lot of work to do that night. There was a whack of homework
to get through, but I'd become quite skilled in convincing
myself that I'd actually get to it "later."

My nightly routine was to respond to each emailer and thank
them for their interest, and offer a vague message of encouragement. Since I was only trying to fix up Leah and Ilana, I
still depended on the rumours of my legendary matchmaking

to circulate so that more guys would contact Matchmaven.

I lay on my bed reviewing the emails, hoping a better match would appear for Leah. I couldn't really update my spreadsheet until the house was empty and I could insert the flash drive into the kitchen computer. The unpleasant smell of the fish cooking wafted into my room, whetting my appetite for food more suitable for a teenager than a black bear. I wandered downstairs to the kitchen to forage for chocolate.

"Oh, I'm glad you're here," Aunt Mira said as she lifted the lid from a pot, releasing a fetid fog into the air. Bubby sipped her seltzer and watched me make my pilgrimage to the pantry. "I have to book a flight for you and Leah for the Saunders bar mitzvah in Brooklyn. I think it's safer to go Thursday night rather than Friday morning. What do you think?"

As if there was any question. "Probably Thursday," I said, as I rooted around for some dried mangos.

"Raina, can you grab me one of those delicious *salt-free* crackers?" Bubby said with a wink. I rolled my eyes and grabbed the box.

"I've also got great news," Mira said. "Uncle Eli is available to tutor you tonight."

"Mrs. Levine strikes again."

"Raina, *please*." Mira glowered and did the dramatically slow exhale thing. You know — the Internationally Recognized Symbol for Disdain. At least with the Bernsteins you always knew where you stood. "Mrs. Levine is trying to help you succeed, and from what she told me this afternoon, it's not happening. She mentioned that you got a 52% on your most recent history paper." She grabbed a pitcher of water from the fridge. "To be honest, spare time isn't always a productive asset for everybody. It can lead to . . . trouble."

Because throwing a party for seniors is the kind of thing that only alienated and rebellious teenagers do. Bubby let out a cough from the kitchen table as she turned the page of a newspaper.

"Rain, I'm more than happy to help you," Eli said as he entered the kitchen, removing his suit jacket.

"It's really not necessary, Uncle Eli." It was less a statement than a plea. "I can manage."

Mira carried the pot to the table. "If Uncle Eli is willing, just be thankful. His time is valuable."

Talk about valuable. The man was a top litigator who billed his clients upward of $600 an hour. This was going to be the most expensive tutoring in recorded history.

"Let's start right after dinner, Rain," he said with a soothing tone as he sat down at the table. "We'll work in my office."

The two hours in his office passed relatively painlessly and included some choice stories about Bubby in her younger days. He also passed along some good news.

"Mira and Leah are moving the computer to the den now," he said.

"Really? Why?"

"We're hoping that it might be a bit quieter for you to do your homework there. Really, Bubby is the only one who spends time there and of course she doesn't use the computer."

I stifled a grin.

"I know what you're thinking, and I agree." He chuckled as he rose from his desk. "Thank *god* she doesn't know how to use a computer."

Eli released me at 9:30 p.m. I bolted to the den where the computer now sat next to the window. Bubby was dozing on the couch, with an old Sox game playing on the television. I instantly recognized the 1975 World Series. It was the bottom of the twelfth inning, which meant that Carlton Fisk was soon going to make some magic.

It was impossible to resist. I landed on the couch, jolting Bubby awake. She yawned, opened her eyes, and glanced at the TV.

"You're just in time," I said.

"Look how lucky," she said. "Raina, go get some chips."

I grimaced. "Bubby, please."

"Oy, don't be so afraid of that aunt of yours!" she said. "Just go get us something to eat."

I reluctantly rose to my feet and trudged to the kitchen. Bubby was a constant predicament in waiting so I searched the pantry for that elusive snack; something tasty but not perilous. Apparently there was no such thing so I just peeled two bananas, cut them into small circles, and arranged them on a paper plate.

I returned to the den just as Fisk was sauntering up to bat, and positioned the plate between us.

Bubby glanced down at the plate. "Monkey food you feed me?" she said with a look of disgust on her face.

"But they're sweet and nutritious!"

"Oh please." She rolled her eyes. "Can you at least get me a beer?"

Mira appeared at the doorway. "Everyone okay? I just finished working on some briefs and I'm going to sleep now."

Mira glanced down at the plate on the couch. "Would you like these sliced bananas, Mira?" Bubby said. "They're sweet and nutritious."

"It's okay, Ma." Mira stepped into the kitchen and disappeared upstairs. Fisk was now poised at the plate. We watched breathlessly as the pitcher wound up. He released the ball and it flew toward home plate.

"I'm having heart palpitations," Bubby called out as she fanned her face with both hands.

Fisk smacked the ball and we watched as he danced to the side and directed the arc of the ball with his arms, willing it to stay inside the foul line.

"Bingo!" Bubby yelled out. I clapped as Fisk's teammates mobbed him.

She nodded and turned to me. "Tell me what's more exhausting then a game-winning home run in the twelfth inning? I'm going to bed." She pulled herself to her feet and tousled my hair.

"Thanks Bubby," I said.

I now had the floor to myself. I sat in front of the computer and opened the Matchmaven account, which was now a portal to the emotional universe of Leah, Daniel, and Ilana. There were two new matchmaking requests. I added them to my database. There were also messages from Leah, Ilana, and — surprise — Jonathan, urging me to set them up. I still hadn't figured out how to inform Daniel that Leah wasn't interested in seeing him again.

There was some serious customer loyalty happening here.

My first goal though was to find someone new for Leah. When the failure of the date with Daniel hit her, she might tailspin into despair. I combed the emails over and over again and frankly couldn't find anyone . . . good enough.

I glanced at the clock on the computer — 11:30 p.m. My arms had grown heavy, my mind was wandering, and I still had an English composition to complete. An instant message came in from Daniel.

Daniel: Maven, Leah was so sweet. Did she say anything?

Maven: Actually, yes. I did talk to her.

Daniel: Excellent! I thought it went really well.

Help.

Maven: It's a bit complicated.

Daniel: Is there a problem? JUST TELL ME.

Maven: It's about the dog.

Daniel: Bronx? You said to do whatever it takes to stay calm as long as I didn't bring my nieces or nephews.

Maven: I did not tell you to bring a dog. You see the problem, Daniel? When a girl goes on a date —

Daniel: Did I blow it?

Maven: — she generally assumes it's with only ONE mammal.

Daniel: I'M SUCH AN IDIOT.

Maven: She said you were nice but you're not for her.

Daniel: Maven, I'm begging you. Please find someone for me.

So here's a rule of thumb. When a grown man uses the word *beg* — you're cooked. What was I supposed to do? I felt like I had no choice so I relented. While I searched through my little database I caught Deb Cohen on Gchat. I felt a bit more confident after Leah's date with Daniel. Leah had liked the man after all; she just wasn't interested in the beast. I typed away, describing Daniel to Deb and confirmed that she was okay with the dude/dog combo.

After I warned Deb about the dog, I warned Daniel about the dog. What I really wanted was to warn the dog about the dog, because he was seriously messing things up for everyone. But everyone was very cooperative so I returned to my English assignment and finished it at 1:30 a.m.

My goal was to find Leah a husband but somehow I was getting sucked into this World Wide Web of Sadness, and it was expanding with each new match. The truth was, the world of Matchmaven was much more compelling and urgent than my schoolwork, which was kind of tanking. And that could be a problem because the more successful I'd be in making matches, the more people would be begging me to help them. In other words, winning for them meant losing for me.

Plus, they were undaunted by my failure. I now had *four* separate people expecting me to make new matches.

The mind of an eligible single is an unknowable one.

> Dear Maven,
>
> Can you help me? I want nothing more than to find a long-term relationship, but I've had so much heartbreak. Unfortunately, I have exceptional looks that tend to intimidate guys. I just moved here from London so maybe I'll have better luck finding a life partner. I'm a financial advisor, forty-seven, blond-haired and blue-eyed. People just assume that I'm thirty, and the truth is that I feel young and find older guys set in their ways and stodgy. I'm looking for a kosher, solid, decent, intelligent, good-looking, interesting, and financially independent guy with a great sense of humour who can deal with my looks.
> Dena

In the past two months I had encountered an ocean of grief and loneliness but I had never really considered the emotional pain of the supermodel. It was touching. Still I *loved* this woman. She was made for Jonathan Sandler. They were two variations on the same theme. They were both extremely self-assured about their abilities and looks. And the beauty of the whole thing was that by the time they stopped lying to each other about their ages, they might already be madly in love. I sent off introductions to both of them.

With Deb, Daniel, Jonathan, and Dena taken care of for now, I had to focus on Ilana and keep my eye open for something great for Leah. I studied the emails. I made a short list, and for Ilana I chose Aaron, the mathematics doctoral student.

I leaned back at the chair and gazed at the stucco ceiling. I still couldn't quite digest how bizarre this was. No matter how unsuccessful the dates were, these people were all *still* begging me to fix them up.

Any doctor with this failure rate would probably lose their medical licence. But apparently, when it comes to fixing up singles, there's no such thing as matchmaking malpractice.

chapter 19

⋙——→ Dogs Tend to Enjoy Eating Disgusting Items ←——⋘

The following Monday, with Leah on the family room computer, and me in my bedroom, I started to step up my plan.

> **Matchmaven:** Leah, Daniel was crazy about you. Guys like you.
>
> **Leah:** Maven, I feel like such a loser.
>
> **Matchmaven:** No, no, no. You're the one of the highest quality people I'm working with.
>
> **Leah:** Really?
>
> **Matchmaven:** Absolutely. How are you adjusting to Toronto?
>
> **Leah:** *Sigh* I'm so lonely. Between work and school I feel so alone.

Like a wrapped package with a pretty bow, here was my opportunity.

> **Matchmaven:** Didn't you say that you used to be really close with your sister?
> **Leah:** We were always best friends.
> **Matchmaven:** So why not reach out to her?
> **Leah:** I don't know. I do miss her.

I clasped my hands to my chest. *Yes!* She was finally coming around.

> **Leah:** But she's given me and my family so much grief. I'm wary.
> **Matchmaven:** Whatever happened, you'll be healthier if you let go of your anger. Maybe it's time to reconcile.
> **Leah:** I'm afraid to trust her.

This was too good to be true. It was so ridiculously *easy* to work on her like this.

> **Matchmaven:** Start slow. You may find that she's matured. Why impose unnecessary loneliness on yourself?
> **Leah:** Maybe.

I leapt onto my bed and jumped. When I was done, I landed on my butt, took a sip of soda water from my night table, and returned to Matchmaven. Deb was online so she gave me the complete scoop.

She and Daniel were now in good shape, even though they got off to a shaky start. Without Bronx along, Daniel was uptight and nervous. But when he'd finished power sweating after the first hour, he calmed down and they enjoyed themselves enough for Deb to agree to another date two nights later. This time, Daniel brought the dog again, explaining to Deb that the vet insisted he not be left alone because Bronx was unwell. Deb sympathized, and the date went smoothly, even when she discovered that the "vet" was actually a dog psychiatrist who was treating Bronx for depression.

That night Deb finally accepted that Daniel and Bronx came as a complete set. Individual parts not for sale.

Just as Deb and I finished instant messaging, "Sweet Caroline," my phone's ring tone, jolted the silence of the room.

"Hi Rain, it's me, Deb," she said.

My breath caught in my throat.

"Listen, I hope you don't mind that I called you," she babbled. "Ilana's my best friend and she told me your name and number, but I promise I won't tell anybody."

A shot of terror pushed me off the bed. "But Ilana said the same thing."

"Please don't worry," Deb said. "I swear neither of us will tell anyone else." My dad was so right. When you tell just one person — it isn't a secret anymore.

"Why are you calling?" I said as I paced the bedroom.

She sighed. "Because I've never felt such happiness in my life and it's all because of you."

I stopped. "Really?"

She was practically singing now. "I know I'm not supposed to have your number but the messaging couldn't convey my gratitude to you. Daniel's *great*!" Her voice was effervescent, like a glass of freshly poured seltzer.

"Cool," I said. I leapt onto my bed and bounced in the air.

"I think he might be my soul mate, but he hasn't hinted at anything. Should I be nervous?"

"No," I said, as I flopped onto my back. "If it's meant to be, then it'll work out at the right time. Trust me."

"You think so?"

"I know so," I said. "In the meantime hang tight and I'll dig around and find out what's going on in his mind."

"I love you, Rain!"

I scratched my jaw. If she only knew.

The next day Dahlia approached me as we filed out of math class. "How's the spreadsheet working out?"

"It's amazing except for the fact that I don't have any privacy at the Bernsteins. They moved the computer, which helps, but Leah uses the printer and Bubby's always in that room."

"Hmm." Dahlia hiked her knapsack over her shoulder. "If you want you can come to my place after school. We can whip up some cookie batter that will *never* see the inside of an oven."

It was the first week of December and this was the first invitation to anyone's house I'd received from someone who wasn't over the age of seventy-five.

"You got me," I said.

Five hours later I was trailing after Dahlia across the marble tiles of her lobby, into a kitchen that must have housed a food preparation business, because it was utterly colossal. I mean, it was epic. There had to be a hundred feet of counter space, miles of hardwood cabinets, industrial-sized stainless steel appliances, and so much granite that somewhere in Italy a quarry must have been stripped clean.

She opened the fridge door. "Sushi or cake batter?"

"What, no compote?"

"If you dare bring up Lillian Shimmel," she said and we both giggled. Dahlia grabbed two Styrofoam trays of sushi from the fridge and set up her laptop on the breakfast nook counter while we settled onto two barstools.

"Feel like working on some math?" Dahlia dug into her bag and scooped out the textbook.

"You're such a bad influence," I groaned as she dropped the book on the counter with a heavy *thwap*. "Do we really have to do that?"

She studied my face, trying to make sense of a member of a non-homework-loving species. "We have a math assignment due tomorrow. Why not?"

"Because I've got . . . bursitis?"

"Forget it, Irving, let's get to work."

We spent the next forty-five minutes working on the math sheet "together" then took a break to whip up some eggless blondies. When the batter was mixed, we returned to the kitchen island with the mixing bowl and two spoons. Dahlia opened her chemistry textbook while I pored over the Matchmaven files.

There was a new request in my account: a message from a woman named Esther.

> Dear Matchmaven,
> I heard that you've succeeded in helping people with challenges and I suppose that as a "senior citizen" I would be considered a "challenge."

Senior citizen?

> I was born and raised in Chicago and was always a strong student. When I completed high school, I had

dreams of becoming a doctor. After I completed a year of undergraduate study, my father died and my mother was diagnosed with MS, so I went home to run the store to support her and my three younger sisters. I attended a community college at night and became an elementary school teacher.

After my mother died, I went to live with an aunt in Toronto. I was single for a long time and had no luck finding a husband until I met the love of my life, Lev. We got married when I was almost thirty and the next six months were the happiest of my life. Tragically, he died suddenly from a brain aneurysm. I never remarried, never had children, and I've been alone most of my life. I know that there's almost no chance that you'd have anyone for me at this age, but I thought I'd try anyways. I really want to believe in second chances. And you have the reputation of being very special.
Esther

Was it me or did it seem like the requests just kept getting sadder? My clients had shown me how much aloneness was out there, but this Esther seemed to be in a class of sorrow that outdid the others.

I tried working on an English assignment, but I had Esther on the brain and it haunted me all evening. When we finished studying at 9:30, Dahlia drove me home. I climbed the stairs to get ready for bed and checked my phone. Daniel was ready to email.

Matchmaven: How's it going with Deb?
Daniel: She's awesome.

Excellent! Now was the time to intervene on Deb's behalf.

> **Matchmaven:** Any thoughts about popping the question?
>
> **Daniel:** All the time.
>
> **Matchmaven:** !!!! So why not just do it?
>
> **Daniel:** One thing is bothering me.
>
> **Matchmaven:** ???
>
> **Daniel:** It's my dog, Bronx. He's extremely intuitive. Almost analytical in how he views people, if you know what I mean.
>
> **Matchmaven:** For sure.
>
> **Daniel:** He's actually brilliant. Anyway, I'm crazy about Deb but why isn't he more excited? He's not responding to her. I don't get it.
>
> **Matchmaven:** So you're saying you need Bronx's blessing.
>
> **Daniel:** Basically, yes. I want to go to the next level with Deb, but this is concerning me.
>
> **Matchmaven:** Well, tell Bronx not to take too long. Deb won't wait around forever.

I certainly wasn't about to wait around either. Immediately, after Daniel and I said goodbye, I called up Deb.

"Deb, I found out what's holding up Daniel," I said breathlessly. "It's the dog."

"I *knew* it," she said. "It's that Brooklyn."

"You mean Bronx?"

"Whatever. Look, it helped Daniel loosen up at first. But that dog *hates* me. It constantly slobbers on me."

"That's what dogs do," I said. "They're like babies with fur glued on."

"Well, this is *targeted* slobbering. And you should see the look he gets in his eyes, Rain. His drool is hostile."

"You're paranoid."

"No, I'm telling you. He bares his teeth at me when Daniel turns away." Her voice darkened. "He pretends to be one thing in front of Daniel, but to me he's a different animal. Rain, I'm just going to come out and say it. *Brutus is a two-faced dog.*"

"Yeah, but he's part of the package, Deb."

"I finally meet a guy I like," she moaned, "and he's got a dog with the integrity of a snake oil salesman."

I could hear her groaning "Why, why, why, why?" as I padded back to the desk and flopped into the chair.

"Maybe Bronx feels threatened by you," I said. "Because Daniel will love *you* more than *him*."

"Get out."

I kicked off my shoes and spun the chair around. "You know what you need to do? You need to win him over. You need to buy that dog a pie or something."

There was silence on the phone. Then a new energy burst out from the other end. "That's it!" she said, her voice ringing with excitement. "I'm going to buy that dog a pie!"

"Well, maybe not an actual pie —"

"No, it's perfect. Botox loves Daniel's food — challah, blueberry muffins, and donuts."

She paused for a second. "Now I understand. Boris has *no idea that he's a dog*!"

"Daniel probably doesn't have the heart to tell him."

"Daniel's going out of town soon and I'm supposed to be taking care of the dog. You know, walking him and feeding him. I'm going to take him a treat!"

"I think Bronx is going to fall in love with you too!" I said. "Especially if you ever get his name right."

"I'm so excited. I'll drop it off when I go to walk him," she said.

Dogs are so easy to solve.

chapter 20
A Match Made in Fenway

Professor K. beckoned me into the kitchen, where the bok choy and cauliflower sat defiantly on the counter next to the juicer. When the juicer finished grinding the vegetables, he handed me my glass. I smiled and raised it to him.

"Why don't you check your mail," he said as he uncovered the aluminum pan. It was filled with Mira's pickled carp and rice.

I swear I'm not making that up.

A really unfortunate cocktail of oxygen, nitrogen, and carp followed me past the ficus tree as I trekked toward the computer.

"I think my plant likes your company," he yelled from the

kitchen. "Ever since you started visiting it's become so robust!"

Which proves my point. Those hideous drinks that he was serving me weren't beverage, they were fertilizer. I inched over to the plant and tipped over my glass. "You're welcome," I whispered to it.

I sank into the chair and contemplated the matchmaking. It was eating up my time, affecting my grades, and putting Mrs. Levine on my tail more than ever. She kept calling my aunt and uncle because I was underperforming. The worst part was that I still hadn't found someone good enough for Leah.

My mind churned and I blankly twisted a lock of hair around my finger as I stared at the ficus. The whole purpose of my secret life was to find Leah a husband, but it had exploded into a full-time effort to help an entire network of individuals who had placed their trust in me and depended on me helping them. They were people with hopes and dreams and lots of pain and they deserved happiness. But still, I was in over my head with this business. If I could only find a fabulous — and willing — matchmaker who could take over my caseload, I'd finally be able to focus on passing my courses.

But I knew that was unrealistic. Because if someone else had been willing to do it, my clients would never have come to me in the first place.

How could I ever have known how complicated and time-consuming matchmaking was? That would partially explain why Mrs. Marmor was so mad at me.

I gazed at the ficus tree, bursting with green foliage thanks to all the vegetable waste I'd been dumping into its soil. And then it occurred to me. That fragile plant was Deb, Daniel, Ilana, and all the others. Even Leah.

And me?

I was the revolting liquid they depended on.

I had no choice. I had to carry on.

I returned to Matchmaven to learn that Ilana and Aaron's date was a disaster. When he came to get her, he started playing a video game with her little brother and wouldn't leave until they finished an hour and a half later. Needless to say, Ilana deserved another date.

Aaron deserved a smack.

And I deserved a break for once.

> **Aaron:** It was a fantastic date. I haven't enjoyed myself this much since my broken relationship with Susan.
>
> **Matchmaven:** I hate to break it to you but it wasn't really a date. You spent most of it playing video games with Ilana's brother.
>
> **Aaron:** Oh. I hadn't thought of that.

There were no new emails so I signed out just as Professor K. emerged from the kitchen. I watched in horror as he carried Mira's dinner spooned out . . . *on two plates.*

He set them up on the dining room table, complete with cutlery and napkins.

"Oh, look at that," he said, noting my emptied glass. "You finished it already. Delicious, isn't it?"

"Um . . . for sure."

"Then let me make you another one." He grabbed the glass and bounded back to the kitchen.

I was defeated. I dropped into the dining room chair and waited for the gag-fest to begin. When he returned with my refill I nibbled on the rice, trying not to choke.

Five parts ketchup, one part Mira-"food."

He dabbed his face with a napkin. "Rain, you look more tired every time I see you."

"It's the schoolwork," I said, rising from my chair to leave, even though I sensed an opportunity to gripe. But I had an English assignment that I was going to have to finally force myself to confront.

"Well instead of going home right away, maybe I could help you."

"I'm good." Time to make my getaway. "I've got a short story to analyze for school."

"Well, hang on," he said, even though it was obvious that *he* was the one hanging on. "Maybe I can help you."

I pursed my lips and pretended to consider it for a few seconds. "It's okay," I said as I picked up my plate. "I have to go home."

"Please," he said. "How else can I thank you?"

The front door was so tantalizingly close.

He gazed at me with his watery eyes. "I insist."

I hesitated. "Sure," I said, dropping back into the chair.

"Which story do you have to analyze?"

"We can choose any short story."

He smacked a fist on the table. "I have the perfect story for you! It's called 'The Lottery.'" He jumped out of his chair, and strode to the living room bookshelf where he retrieved an ancient-looking book. A musty odour rose from its pages when he opened them to the correct spot. "Do you want to read, or should I?" he said.

I waved my hand. "It's okay, I don't need to read."

I clutched my purse and pulled my cell phone out. I was tired and just wanted to go home. At this point, I could do nothing but wait it out.

"The flowers were blossoming profusely and the grass was richly green . . ." he read. I glanced at the cell phone sitting discreetly on my knee. No messages or texts. Matchmaven was quiet tonight.

". . . Bobby Martin had already stuffed his pockets full of stones . . ."

I leaned back on the chair and closed my eyes and listened to his reedy voice fill the air around us.

" . . . there was a great deal of fussing to be done before Mr. Summers declared the lottery open . . ."

Apparently the village people were preparing for a ritual. It was a lottery but there was something disturbing about it.

"The crowd was quiet. A girl whispered, 'I hope it's not Nancy,' and the sound of the whisper reached the edges of the crowd."

There was something menacing about the story. I opened my eyes and watched Professor K. read from the book.

"Although the villagers had forgotten the ritual and lost the original black box, they still remembered to use stones."

Suddenly it seemed that Professor K. wasn't reading quickly enough. Tessie Hutchinson had now picked the slip of paper from the black box with the black spot on it and the entire village was ready with their stones.

Was this really how it was going to end?

Professor K. continued reading and finally reached the last horrible, tragic, and cruel line of the story.

"'It isn't fair, it isn't right,' Mrs. Hutchinson screamed, and then they were upon her."

I let out a gasp.

"Terrible, isn't it?" he said in a quiet voice.

It was a horror movie.

"What does it mean?" I stuttered. "They just choose someone to be stoned to death every year?"

He smiled. "Ahh. Let's figure that out." It was like

Professor K. was *enjoying* a horror movie.

But he was so old.

We spoke about religion. We spoke about rituals. We spoke about ritual without meaning. About conformity. About the depravity of human nature. We were so immersed in Shirley Jackson's world that I didn't notice how much time had passed until ten, when I bid him goodbye, slid into the car, and motored home.

As I headed toward the stairs, Leah popped out of her bedroom, wearing wine-coloured hospital scrubs. I felt my shoulders tense, as they always did when we bumped into each other. Leah glanced at her watch and shot me a suspicious look.

"I was hanging out with Professor K.," I said.

"Until ten?"

"We were reading a short story together. It was so interesting."

"Really?" She skipped down the stairs until we stood side by side. "The whole evening?"

I nodded. "We discussed it for hours."

She cocked her head to the side and studied me.

"He's nice," I said with a shrug.

She began to turn away. Then she stopped, reached out, and gently squeezed my arm. "I'm proud of you."

I bounced up the stairs, closed my door, and I leapt onto my bed.

Things only got better when I opened the computer and saw I had a new email.

From Leah's future husband.

Dear Matchmaven,

I heard you do good work as a matchmaker. I'm a twenty-
seven-year-old civil engineer. I was engaged, but my fiancée
broke it off a year ago and to be honest it's taken a long
time to get over her. I like to run, play basketball, and
baseball. I'm originally from Boston but moved to Toronto
after graduating from McGill University.

I'm pretty chilled with a good sense of humour. I'm
looking for someone beautiful, smart, kind, and open. Can
you help me?

Best regards,

Jake Marks

Can I help you? He was from *Boston* and played *baseball*. I tried
not to get too blinded by his glorious Red Soxiness. He was
successful. He was physically fit, like Leah. He was the right age.

I emailed him right away.

It was a match made in Fenway!

chapter 21

➤➤➤ No Earthy Dog-Guy ←←←

Over the next week and a half, Leah and Jake had four really good, long phone conversations. She stopped averting her eyes when she saw me and even smiled a few times.

On Sunday night I sat at the computer scrolling through Matchmaven while Bubby dozed on the couch in front of a DVD playing an episode of the *Flip Wilson Show*, circa 1971. An hour and a half before their date, a message popped up from Jake. It was a great opportunity to pry him for his preferences as well as promote Leah as the incredible catch that she was.

Jake: I'm really excited to meet Leah.

Matchmaven: Have you thought about where you're going to take her?

Jake: Sheraton Parkway in Richmond Hill. It's pretty and I think they might have an excellent goldfish pond.

Matchmaven: I love an excellent goldfish pond.

Jake: Exactly.

Matchmaven: What's the dress code?

Jake: Sophisticated. I'll be honest; I don't understand when women don't take care of themselves.

Matchmaven: I know.

Matchmaven: What do you mean?

Jake: I just mean putting a bit of effort into how they dress. Especially on a date.

Matchmaven: I agree.

Which meant that I had to convince Leah to do a 180. This time she'd have to dress exactly opposite from her last date. Jake was no earthy dog-guy. He sounded like a sophisticated man.

With ninety minutes until Jake arrived, I found myself on high alert. It was particularly significant because it was the first anniversary of the day she started dating Ben. This time though, Mira and Eli wouldn't be able to greet Jake and invite him in for the five-minute interrogation. Mira had a meeting and Eli was working late at his office.

I sat at the computer desk in the den, combing through MazelTovNation when a notice caught my eye.

Jonathan Sandler and Dena Shore were engaged!

That was my match! I hooted out loud.

"Do you know them?"

I spun around in my chair. Leah stood behind me, wearing

a bathrobe. Why was she always there whenever someone got engaged?

She pointed at the huge picture of Jonathan and Dena standing in front of a huge Mylar balloon that said *mazel tov* on the monitor. "How would you know them?" she said.

"I think . . . she was a division head in camp," I said. Three decades ago, maybe. Certainly not in my lifetime.

"Anyway," she said. "I'm . . . going out tonight. Can I borrow some clothes?"

"No problem!" I rolled back the chair and sprang up the stairs to my bedroom. I threw open my closet door. "Is this like a date or something?"

"Rain, please," she said as she peered inside. Stung, I just nodded. We gazed at the inside of the cupboard where my clothes hung neatly in categories — skirts, blouses, dresses, and sweaters. We studied the contents carefully, moving hangers as we appraised the possibilities.

"Michael Kors, von Fürstenberg, Kenneth Cole," I said, pointing to three skirts.

"Ralph Lauren, Donna Karan, Zac Posen," she said, as she gestured to three blouses.

"Kors," I said.

"Lauren?"

"Posen."

It was settled. When it came down to it, Leah and I spoke the same language.

"Thanks, Rain," she said as she pulled a beige shell over her head.

"You should wear heels too," I said. Thankfully, a mini-thaw in the weather had melted the snow enough to wear shoes on the sidewalks.

She stopped with her arms mid-air and looked at me strangely. "Didn't you tell me to wear flats last time?"

"I'm just going by this outfit," I said as I pointed to her. "I think you need something a bit more formal on your feet."

"Well, okay. I guess I'll trust your fashion sense." She tugged down the waist of the shell, and then slipped on a floaty emerald blouse. "Thanks, Rain," she said. "I appreciate this."

"No problem. Do you want me to answer the door, when he comes?"

She sighed. "Okay, fine. But just say hello to him and then get me right away. Okay?"

"You can trust me," I said.

Because that's all I really wanted.

Jake was a looker, alright. Bubby obviously thought so too, because when I opened the door, she somehow was standing right behind me, gasping in my ear. With sandy-coloured hair, chiseled cheekbones, and clear jade eyes, it was hard to turn away from him. But true to my word I just said hello.

"I'm waiting for Mrs. Feldman," Bubby claimed as she stubbornly stood her ground at the front door while I flew up the stairs to retrieve Leah.

As they left, I tiptoed to the catwalk at the front of the hall and peeked out the window just as Jake opened the car door for Leah. Good sign. Once they drove off, I paced the hall upstairs. Leah didn't seem quite as terrified this time. The date with Daniel had definitely given her some practice and loosened her up a bit.

I finally went down to the kitchen to drown my anxiety in

ketchup chips. Bubby and Mrs. Feldman were both settled on the family room couch watching an episode of the *Mod Squad* (circa 1969) on the DVD player in the den. I sat at the kitchen table and pretended to focus on quadratic equations. Did I mention that I hate quadratic equations and that they're ugly and stupid and that I don't even agree with them?

Bubby and Mrs. Feldman were now engaged in an animated discussion about somebody named Linc. I whipped out my phone and dialled Dahlia. "I need you. Will you come over? I've got some great ketchup chips here."

The voices in the den grew louder now as the two women obviously could not see eye to eye about a forty-five-year-old cop show about hippies.

"Now?" Dahlia said. "It's kind of late."

I decided to sweeten the pot, "And I really need help with my quadratic equations."

"Ooh, such temptation," she said. "But what's that noise?"

"Noise?" I covered the phone and fled from the kitchen where Mrs. Feldman's voice wouldn't carry. "What noise?"

"Wait a minute," Dahlia said. "Mrs. Feldman is there, isn't she?"

"Help me."

"Nice try," Dahlia said. "Those ladies are legitimately scary."

I sighed and pretended to work on my homework. Every minute passed like an hour. At 9 p.m. Bubby announced that she was going to sleep and Mrs. Feldman clipped her way out to her car. At 10:30 the front door finally opened. Four and a half hours was a promising first date. It was soon clear though that the footsteps approaching the kitchen were not high heels on the marble floor. I sank back in my seat.

"Hi, sweetie," Mira said as she dropped her briefcase onto

a kitchen chair. "I've got loads of groceries still sitting in the car. Will you bring them in?"

She lowered her voice to a whisper and looked around her. "Is Leah home?"

"Not yet."

"Let's keep our fingers crossed." She removed her down coat and threw it over a chair.

The front door immediately opened again and Leah swished into the kitchen.

Mira turned to her with outstretched arms. "How was it, honey?"

Leah nodded slowly with a cryptic smile on her face. "I'm a bit afraid to talk about it, Aunt Mira."

"I understand," Mira said. "I'm sure you'll have a good discussion with that lovely matchmaker. What's her name? Matchster?"

"Matchmaven." Leah giggled.

"I've never heard of an anonymous matchmaker," Mira said, shaking her head. "But people are saying that she really knows what she's doing."

My heart palpitated.

"She's pretty awesome," Leah said. "Aunt Mira, do you mind if I go message Matchmaven from my laptop upstairs?" Mira nodded with a smile. Leah slipped off her heels and padded toward the stairs. I jumped out of the seat to race up to my room. "The groceries, Rain," Mira said.

I stumbled mid-stride. "Aunt Mira, I have to finish my math. Can't it wait?"

She leaned her head to the side and pulled out her earring. "It'll take five minutes. And I need you to put them away too."

I threw on my ski jacket, dashed out to Mira's Camry, and was aghast to find it brimming with bright yellow supermarket bags. Like she was catering a wedding, or something. It actually took me twenty minutes to haul in the bags and fit everything into the fridge and pantry.

I finally bolted up the stairs, slammed the door shut, and opened my phone.

> Hi Matchmaven,
> I wish I could talk to you in person. I have so many thoughts about Jake and I'd love to hash it out with you. Let's be in touch tomorrow. Thanks for your incredible help!
> Leah

I kicked the mattress beneath me. What was she talking about? *How did it go?* Why couldn't I just run down the hall and *talk*? Like I used to when she was first dating Ben. We'd dissect each date for two hours.

And then the next day we'd do it all over again.

Dahlia and I claimed a table at the back of the school's cafeteria so she could spread out her chemistry notes. A microwave on the shelf behind us blasted out rays of fishitude, reminding me that Mira's dinner was only hours away. I nibbled a baby carrot while pulling out my cell phone.

"I'd put that thing away, if I were you," Dahlia said, as she turned a page in her textbook.

"I have to know how Leah's date went." I opened Matchmaven and placed the cell on my knee.

"Mrs. Levine is lurking," she said, pushing her glasses up her nose.

"I'll be careful," I said. Sure enough Leah was there.

> **Leah:** Jake is good-looking, smart, and personable. I'd like to see him again.
>
> **Matchmaven:** Excellent! Any concerns?
>
> **Leah:** I was slightly uncomfortable that he brought up his ex-fiancée twice.
>
> **Matchmaven:** Hmmm. They broke up six months ago?
>
> **Leah:** A year.
>
> **Matchmaven:** Red flag.
>
> **Leah:** But he's so good-looking.
>
> **Matchmaven:** BRIGHT red flag.
>
> **Leah:** I like him.
>
> **Matchmaven:** Okay, go out again, but be cautious.
>
> **Leah:** You're so wise. I wish I could meet you.

Me too.

> **Matchmaven:** You'd be disappointed.
>
> **Leah:** No, really, can we meet? I have no one to tell anyway!
>
> **Matchmaven:** If I was exposed I wouldn't be able to help you anymore.
>
> **Leah:** That's no good. I don't want to lose you — you're my only friend in Toronto.
>
> **Matchmaven:** That's not true. You have family.
>
> **Leah:** It's not the same as friends.
>
> **Matchmaven:** Maybe it's time to repair that friendship with your sister.

Leah: Maybe. She can be so kind — like lending me clothes for my date and she visits this old professor.

Matchmaven: So what's the problem? You could have a built-in friend right at your aunt's house!

Leah: It's just that I don't quite trust her. She was mean and insulting about my makeup before my date with Daniel. What's more worrisome is that I feel like she's up to something. She just disappeared one night. She eventually showed up at midnight claiming she was on a school project but I'm pretty sure I saw her hanging out at the park. And when we were at an engagement party she literally spied on me in the bathroom all evening.

I blanched.

This was so much worse than I thought. I squeezed my eyes shut and the din of the cafeteria faded. I needed to focus my mind and figure out a way to salvage this situation.

But of course I could — I was being given a chance to defend myself! And defend I did.

Matchmaven: First of all, never ever assume you know all sides to a story. Second, I think you have to ask yourself if you care about her or not. And if you do, then you need to reach out so that if she is in trouble, you can help her. And third? Consider that even though you're upset about being on the dating market again, maybe you really weren't meant to marry Ben.

Leah: Can you be my wise woman?

Matchmaven: Letting go can be very liberating.

Leah: I gotta say: I like you. ☺

Matchmaven: I like you too. ☺

I closed my eyes again and images of a future with my sister flooded in. A weekend at the Saunders bar mitzvah in New York together: shopping, eating out, and visiting friends. And, of course, Leah finding true love.

Dahlia elbowed me but it was too late.

"Your phone."

Mrs. Levine was towering over me. I let out a tiny gasp.

"You know the rules," she said. "You *signed* a form indicating that you read the student handbook."

Three girls at the next table turned around to check out the action. My shoulders slumped. "I won't do it again," I mumbled. "I forgot."

"It's rather *unfortunate* that you gave yourself permission to break school rules in such a brazen way."

Silence rippled like waves around Mrs. Levine and rolled across the cafeteria. I gulped. "I'll close it," I said, as I quickly exited Matchmaven. "I'm really sorry."

"If it happens again, I'll confiscate it. For a month."

She resumed her patrol of the cafeteria.

Dahlia was annoyed. "Everyone has phones. Why is she picking on you?"

"Now I can't get anything done until after school."

"No problem. You'll come home with me and I'll help you."

chapter 22

⇒⟶ A State of Esther ⟵⟪

We set up camp on the Persian rug in Dahlia's family room, surrounded by Nibs, Oreos, and ketchup chips, completely strung out on trans fats. Tonight Matchmaven had only one new message. It was from Esther, who'd become a bit of a pen pal. I know this sounds awful, but I found myself strangely compelled by the sadness of her life. It was like corresponding with a character in a tragic film. Her name on the email address was very cryptic, "Esther LLLevad." She probably didn't want anyone to know that she was doing this.

> Dear Matchmaven,
>
> I gather from your comments that you might be much

younger than me? I never did, but I really do believe in second chances now. Life seemed so full of promise when I married — Lev was born in a displaced persons camp in Germany in 1945. His parents survived the Holocaust and moved to North America in 1948. They were extremely protective of him. After they objected to us moving to Minnesota, where Lev was offered an academic position, I vented to him. Unfortunately, his parents heard. They became so concerned about breaking up our marriage that they stopped visiting us, no matter how much we reassured them. His father had a tumour diagnosed six weeks after that. The family was devastated, and a month later Lev had the aneurysm.

I tried apologizing to his mother but she wouldn't have anything to do with me anymore. I should never have given up. That's the great regret of my life. I should have done everything in my power to make amends while I still had the opportunity.

All I have left of Lev are photographs, memories, and a beautiful necklace that he had designed especially for me: three rubies on a gold pendant in the shape of an elephant with my Hebrew name "Esther" engraved. The ancient Hebrew word for elephant, "Peel" comes from "pelah": wonder. Finding each other filled us both with wonder.

Anyway, I've been doing all the talking. I know you don't like to divulge any information about yourself, but I'd love to hear a bit about you.
Esther

It wasn't just the tragedy in her letters, it was the regret. Knowing that all it takes is a few hours — even a few minutes.

And then you've got decades of grief.

Esther had been alone almost her entire life and that sorrow came out in every sentence of her letters. I mean, I thought of my clients and the longing in their emails. It was probably a safe assumption that almost every one of those individuals had an image in their mind that kept them up at night, and drove them to continue dating, even after their hearts were broken by rejection, humiliation, and despair. And that image was ending up alone and lonely for the rest of their lives.

I'm pretty sure that image was Esther. Or maybe it was another image and this wasn't the first time I'd encountered it, but it was possibly the first time I understood it. I cringed at the thought of the teacher that had wandered the halls of my old school, Maimonides, like a ghost. Mr. Sacks's wife had died the year before I started Maimonides. When he taught my ninth grade chemistry class, he muttered, and had no energy. He shuffled across the halls like his soul was gone but his body still lingered. And his memory lapses were pretty bad. I cringed at how amusing we found them at the time. People had said Mr. Sacks hadn't really survived his wife's death.

Not every single person existed in a state of Esther. But Mr. Sacks did.

Esther desperately needed a partner and the answer to her loneliness came to me like a bolt of lightning.

Clearly I had to set her up with Mr. Sacks.

This was going to be a bit tricky. Just thinking about him made me queasy. How could I possibly approach the man? I had humiliated him.

He hated me.

And then there was Esther with her regret of a lifetime.

I had to fix them up.

Which was ridiculous. *He hated me.*

I cringed at the thought of how disgusted with me he must have been. I'd never even personally apologized to him. Those stupid, stupid emails I'd sent had resulted in the most humiliating expulsion from Maimonides and the final straw for my ex-future-brother-in-law. Maybe Ben had a point in wanting to have nothing to do with our family anymore. I'd gotten kicked out of school, but still my family had protected me, tried to shield me from the consequences of my choices. And when they did that for me, I'd shamed them even worse.

"Are you okay?" Dahlia dropped to the carpet and offered me hearts of palms — straight from the can.

I shook my head. "I just need to finish an email."

"You sure?" Dahlia watched me as I read Esther's letter again. In some ways I was a recovering Esther too, after all those school moves with only a sister as my friend. It had created an insatiable social appetite in me by the time I got to high school. In ninth grade I transformed myself from "out" girl to "it" girl. I went from being a decent student to a pretty awful one. Maybe that was the reason I couldn't stand Mr. Sacks. Every day, he'd radiated the loneliness that I'd been running away from in the years before high school.

Was it worth it to go through life regretting not fixing things like Esther?

Forget matches. Setting up Mr. Sacks was nowhere near my place. There was something far more important that I needed to do.

"Dahlia, I really, *really* hurt my teacher in New York."

"It's bothering you now, because . . . ?"

"He's old and I think frail."

"Can you email him?"

"No. No. I can't."

"Okay, just wait here a minute."

"She climbed to her feet and pattered out of the family room, returning a minute later carrying a stationery box. She placed it in front of me and dropped a pen next to it. I opened the box and lifted up a piece of baby blue stationery and started to write.

Dear Mr. Sacks . . .

Apologies are complicated things.

If you apologize immediately after you've hurt someone then you're probably trying to make them feel better. You feel bad because they feel bad.

But what if you wait and only apologize after weeks of remorse? Or months? Maybe you're just doing it to unburden yourself of uncomfortable feelings like guilt or embarrassment. In other words, you're not doing it so much to make your victim feel better. You're doing it to make yourself feel better.

It had been almost half a year since I sat down in the computer lab and discovered that Mr. Sacks — old, boring, and burnt-out — hadn't logged off his computer. The principal, Rabbi Singer, might not have reacted so harshly if I'd been a better student. A better person. But the truth was that, after traipsing from city to city, arriving at Maimonides was an all-you-can-eat buffet of cell phone minutes, sleepovers, and shopping outings with friends.

What could I do? New York called to me. I always had a friend to sneak off with to ball games, to shop, or to explore

Manhattan. I had essentially become a part-time student. But even that wouldn't have been enough to warrant an expulsion. It was those dead-on imitations of Mr. Sacks that won me more friends, but appalled the school. Especially when Mr. Sacks caught me doing it.

By the time I got into Mr. Sacks's email account last June, the school was more than happy to get rid of me.

I was probably like Bubby at the Shalom Gardens — not exactly an asset at that point. Given the amount of time that had passed, this apology was probably a tainted one. The Sacks family already had months for their shock to gel into a solid mould of disgust.

But the image of Esther chafed. What are you supposed to do with your regrets when you're old and it's too late to do anything about it? How come I didn't write him right away? Why hadn't I begged him for forgiveness immediately?

What was I thinking?

Dahlia rolled over on the carpet and watched me write out a letter in longhand.

"He must be really old, if you're writing a letter by hand," she said as she peered over my shoulder.

"He is, but I kind of messed with his email account so I don't want to apologize that way." I pointed up at her computer. "Can you look up his address? Mordechai Sacks."

She sauntered to the computer and typed in U.S. White Pages. When we were done, she drove me to the post office and I mailed off my letter to Mr. Sacks by Priority post. I figured that it would take at least a week until I heard back from him.

If I heard back.

chapter 23

≫——→ A Beagle Named Chaucer ←——≪

The scent of freshly baked oatmeal raisin cookies teased the insides of Leah's Saturn as we motored through a thick haze of snowflakes toward Professor K.'s house. Between three additional dates with Jake and Matchmaven's encouragement, things were finally defrosting between us. Happy new Leah had even suggested this visit and baked for the occasion.

I'm still not sure I trusted Jake, but I'd learned my lesson. This time I was going to keep my mouth shut. And maybe *I* was the problem because nobody was good enough for Leah.

"What do you talk to the professor about?" Leah adjusted the rear-view mirror.

"Literature."

She grinned. "Really?"

"Honestly, he should be teaching at Moriah," I said. "He's so interesting."

She shook her head.

"Leah," I leaned back on the headrest. "Can I ask how it's going with that boy you're dating?"

"It's good." She pressed her lips together to hold back a smile.

"That's great! Did you —?"

"Rain, I need my privacy this time," she said with a slight edge. "So let's just allow me to handle my dating life."

I fell silent. She reached out and squeezed my knee. "Okay?"

I nodded, waiting for the pit in my stomach to disappear.

When we arrived at Professor K.'s, he wasted no time ushering Leah directly to the juicer. I half suspected he was going to puree the cookies too but he stuck with purple cabbage. I slipped into a bathroom that looked suspiciously like a time capsule from Jonathan Sandler's toddlerhood. The toilet and sink were burgundy and the wall tiles were shiny, pink, and cracked. I turned on my phone to check my email. There was only one short message from Leah, raving about Jake.

When I sauntered back to the living room, I found Leah on the plastic couch sipping her cabbage. She was describing her work at the hospice to Professor K., who really was an excellent listener. I dropped onto the couch next to her.

When she finished, Professor K. rose from his easy chair. "Would you like to see some pictures?" he said.

"I'd love to," she said, her face crinkling with a smile. Professor K. wandered to a bookshelf and rummaged through the bottom shelf.

"He's so charming," she whispered. I nodded in agreement. The guy was definitely a find.

Professor K. soon returned to his easy chair and flipped through pages of black-and-white photos in an ancient album.

"That's my Rose," Professor K. said, pointing to a photograph of a short woman with a dog standing on the sidewalk in front of Maple Leaf Gardens. "She also was an avid reader."

Rose wore large black spectacles, like an accidental 1950s hipster.

"And what a cute dog," Leah said.

"A sweet little beagle named Chaucer," he said. Leah leafed through the pages of the album while Professor K. provided running commentary on Chaucer, his late wife, his children, and grandchildren. When it was done, she handed the album back to him.

"You have quite a book collection," Leah said, pointing to the shelves.

"We loved reading together. Newspapers too," he said. "We started getting delivery of the *New York Times* from the year we were married. My Rose did the Sunday crossword puzzle in pen in no time."

The *New York Times*? Esther had mentioned that also.

I surveyed his living room. The room shouted books! Reading! Education! Why had it taken me this long to think of this?

"I don't believe it," I muttered. My heart raced with excitement. Professor K. wasn't that much older than Esther. My priority with Mr. Sacks was the apology.

For Professor K. it was going to be *love*!

I unsuctioned my hand from the plastic couch and edged over to the computer desk. Yes, it was risky with both of them sitting right there, but excitement defeated caution. I grabbed my purse and excavated until I found Professor K.'s business card, complete with email address, sitting under weeks of clutter.

> Dear Professor Kellman,
>
> I don't know if you've heard of me, but I've heard wonderful things about you. I've made some pretty interesting matches over the last few months. I have a lovely client whom I think you'd really like. She's an educated, intelligent, and insightful woman. She's kind and elegant. If you're interested, I'd be happy to arrange a match.
>
> Yours truly,
>
> Matchmaven

I hit the send button and sat back in the chair. Was it even possible to fall in love in your sixties or seventies? I'd have said no. I mean, think about it. When was the last time you saw that happen in a movie?

When it comes to age, people make no sense. If someone dies in their seventies everyone acts like it's the most freakish thing in the world. How unnatural! "Oh, but she was so *young*!" they'll say. But when my mother turned forty she moped about being old for a week. So apparently you're old in middle age, but when you grow older you become young again.

Please don't ask me to explain that.

Either way, if this match worked out, it would be magic.

Professor K.'s response came that night.

Dear Matchmaven,

I was surprised to receive your suggestion for a match, but this woman sounds lovely. I'd like to take you up on your offer.

Sincerely,

Mo Kellman

Woohoo! Who knew about the thrill of retirement romance!

chapter 24
Re-finding Leah

Professor K. and Esther were an item! It was a fantastic beginning to the new year.

I huddled in the school bathroom and read Esther's email.

Dear Matchmaven,

First of all, thanks so much for your advice about the black blazer. I wore it on last night's date with the grey blouse as you suggested. I also wore something that I haven't put on in almost thirty years: the gold elephant necklace with the three rubies on it and my name engraved in Hebrew. The gift from Lev was so precious but I've felt too guilty to wear it. Mo even commented about the necklace — it is of course, an extremely unusual piece.

Mo has given me a second chance at happiness. The last two weeks with him have been like a dream. No matter how long our conversations are, it never feels like there's enough time.

How are things going with you? I'm so glad you shared a little bit about yourself in your last email, even if it was only what you called a "rant." Is that woman you work with still giving you a hard time? All we can do is try to feel compassion and offer a helping hand.

With gratitude,

Esther

Between Tamara and Jeremy, Leah and Jake, Esther and Professor K., Deb and Daniel, Jonathan and Dena, I was brimming with love. Right?

Actually not. As thrilled as I was by Esther's relationship with the professor, her emails left me with a nagging sense of melancholy.

My problems with Leah were a reflection of my behaviour. Specifically with Mr. Sacks. I was overcome with regret. I'd never considered the expiry date tagged on to the time you get to make amends. And then if you miss your chance you're haunted forever by something that's never going to go away and can never be fixed.

I shuddered and checked my watch, measuring time until school was over.

When I arrived at home, I headed straight for Mira's mailbox. I found a flyer for a local tanning salon, two bills, and a cream-coloured envelope for a wedding invitation in Montreal.

There was still no response from Mr. Sacks.

I had to face the fact that he was not going to answer my letter. And why should he? What positive thing had I ever done for him?

It was time to try apologizing again, although maybe he'd think I was stalking him if I sent another letter.

That's when the realization hit.

I was going to be in New York for the Saunders bar mitzvah in a few weeks.

I would visit Mr. Sacks and apologize in person!

I commanded myself to be happy when I got the big email from Jake, but I wasn't having any of it. Maybe nobody would ever be good enough for my sister.

No matter. Silence was my new philosophy.

> Hi Matchmaven,
>
> Leah is great. Don't say anything, but I'm really into her. She's gorgeous and stylish and lovely. I want to take her out for dinner tonight and then back to the Sheraton Parkway for drinks since that's where our first date was. I want tonight to be meaningful.
>
> I'll be in touch,
>
> Best,
>
> Jake

Meaningful?

That could mean only one thing.

Jake was going to propose.

Dear Leah,

I hope you're all ready for tonight's date. I think Jake really likes you! Just remember that when it comes to big decisions always listen to your gut. You have your whole life ahead of you.

Xoxo

Matchmaven

Was that neutral enough?

Leah was happy. This was good. Happy Leah borrowed my clothes. Happy Leah smiled at me and complimented me on my friendship with Professor K. Happy Leah even admitted to me that she was seeing someone "special."

The night of the "meaningful" date there was a knock on my bedroom door.

"Listen, don't ask me questions, okay?" It was Leah. Her hair was pulled back in a half bun, with strands of hair trailing down her cheeks. "I'm going out tonight and I need you to answer the door again."

I clapped my hands together and grinned. "No problem." Mira and Eli were in Stratford for the night so I was promoted to butler.

"No talking to him, okay?" she said as she pushed a butter-fly clasp onto the back of her earring.

"Not a word," I said.

"Also, Bubby's gawking is embarrassing," she said. "Would it be possible to keep her away from him too?"

"No."

"I guess that's too much to ask. So how do I look?" she said, twirling around, her gathered skirt floating in a circle around her.

"Beautiful," I said.

The doorbell rang and I bounded down the stairs.

"Hi, I didn't introduce myself last time," I said. "I'm Leah's sister, Rain."

"Nice to meet you," he said. "I'm Jake." His was a smile that dazzled.

"I'm Bubby," a voice behind me boomed out. "You want some marble cake, maybe?"

"That's so incredibly kind of you," he said to a beaming Bubby. "I'm not hungry now though."

"I'll go get her," I said. I bolted up the stairs where Leah peaked over the railing, just out of eyesight.

"He's cute," I whispered.

"I know," she said, hoisting a Zara bag over her shoulder. "Wish me luck."

"What are you doing with this?" I said, grabbing the bag.

"My scrubs," she said. "I have a midnight shift, so Jake is going to drop me off at the hospice after the date."

"Someone's feeling comfortable!" I said with the rush of a thrill.

She pecked me on the cheek and bounced down the stairs. When the front door clicked shut I leapt on my bed and started jumping.

Leah was re-finding love.

And I was re-finding Leah.

I parked myself in front of the computer, with Matchmaven shamelessly open. It had become obvious that Bubby, who was watching an old Blue Jays rerun, was oblivious to everything I was doing on the computer.

I had two assignments and three tests to contend with in the next three days. I was at the point where just passing would be good enough. Professor K. was going to edit my English paper on Faulkner, so I had to pick that up later.

The entire semester had been an academic bust. I had become so addicted to matchmaking that I think I'd pretty much confirmed Mrs. Levine's worst fears about me.

An hour into wrestling with a math assignment, an instant message popped on the screen.

> **Leah:** You there, Maven?
> **Matchmaven:** Yes!!!!
> **Leah:** Engaged.

I jumped out of my seat. Leah's engaged!

> **Leah:** Jake's engaged.
> **Matchmaven:** MAZEL TOV!!!!!!

Wait. *Jake's* engaged?

> **Matchmaven:** WHAT ARE YOU SAYING?
> **Leah:** JAKE GOT ENGAGED TO HIS EX
> **Matchmaven:** WHEN?
> **Leah:** JUST NOW.
> **Matchmaven:** WHAT ARE YOU TALKING ABOUT? CAN WE STOP SHOUTING?
> **Leah:** He got a phone call and disappeared for forty minutes while I sat there like an IDIOT. Then he came back and announced that he was engaged. You warned me to be cautious. I should have listened.

The tears that sprang from my eyes at that moment were not your basic single-purpose ones. No, I was burning with pain and anger. And hatred.

How *dare* he?

> **Matchmaven:** I could strangle him. I'm so sorry. You don't deserve this.

Leah wasn't responding now.

> **Matchmaven:** Are you there? Where are you?
>
> **Leah:** I'm bawling in the bathroom at the Sheraton Parkway in Richmond Hill. He offered to drive me to the hospice but I told him to get lost. I don't have any money, and my credit card is at home. All I have is one token for the subway ride home.
>
> **Matchmaven:** I'd bring you money but I don't have a car.
>
> **Leah:** What should I do?
>
> **Matchmaven:** Call your aunt and uncle.
>
> **Leah:** They're out of town.
>
> **Matchmaven:** Get your sister.
>
> **Leah:** No! My car is all I have left and she dented it the day after I got it.

The truth was that ever since I dinged her car I wasn't even allowed to *look* at it without sunglasses.

> **Leah:** Please, this is the worst night of my life.

A vein on my forehead throbbed like it was going to explode out of my skin. Mira and Eli were in Stratford, Bubby didn't drive, and Leah didn't have any friends in Toronto. We were both stuck in a city that we didn't want to be in. I had to get to her. This was the worst night of our life.

I had no way of getting there.

Mira's car was in for repairs, Eli's Volvo was with them in Stratford, and I wasn't going near Leah's car.

I dialled Dahlia. She was at her cousin's birthday party reception.

I searched for directions to the Sheraton Parkway online, but it was at the corner of Highway 7 and Nowhere. A quick internet search warned me that public transit would take all evening. I called up a car service and was told to expect to pay $40 in each direction, not including a tip. I paced the kitchen in terror. Bubby seemed to be in a near-catatonic state. Think, think. I ran my fingers through my hair, and tried to calm myself down.

> **Leah:** I feel like my life has slipped away and I'm hanging
> by a thread. You're that thread, Maven.

I eased myself onto the couch next to Bubby. I needed to calm myself down in order to come up with a solution and what could be more hypnotic then watching a minute of the Blue Jays? I exhaled slowly, trying to tame my racing pulse.

"What's wrong with you," Bubby said.

"Nothing. I'm okay."

"Ach, these shmoes are making me crazy," she said, pointing at the TV. "They should just bring back Cito Gaston."

"They losing again?"

"They don't have to!"

I exhaled a slow breath and counted to six. My heart felt

like it was going to blow up. How on earth could I get Leah the money?

The game wasn't calming me down. "How can you watch them, Bubby?" I said.

She shrugged. "Nothing else is on."

What was I supposed to do about Leah?

"See, these Jays need to take a lesson from history," Bubby said with disgust. "Remember Dave Roberts?"

I knew exactly what she meant. "The Sox are down four to three in the top of the ninth and he steals a base off the Yankees."

"And look at that amazing comeback."

"And finally, an end to the Curse of the Bambino," I said.

"Oh, would you just *steal second* already!" she yelled at the TV.

It was a light bulb moment. I jumped off the couch and scurried back to the computer.

I had no choice.

> **Matchmaven:** I'm coming.
> **Leah:** You're an angel.

I had to borrow Leah's car.

> **Matchmaven:** I care about you. But I must remain anony-
> mous.
> **Leah:** Please just help me. I'll look at a magazine so I won't
> see you.
> **Matchmaven:** Okay. I'll figure out a place to leave the
> money then I'll message you.

Leaving her the money would be another challenge.

I had to get there first. I didn't have money for her plus $80 and change for a taxi. But I couldn't make her wait while I took a bus all night.

> **Matchmaven:** Promise not to even look for my car. I want
> to continue working with you, but I can't be betrayed.
> **Leah:** I would never betray you.

I printed out driving directions to the hotel.

"Bubby, I'm going to crash upstairs," I said.

"Sure you are," she said, her eyes still glued to the TV.

I flew to Leah's bedroom where I found the car keys in a ceramic bowl on her desk. Two minutes later I tiptoed out the front door and backed out of the driveway. The car purred quietly as I inched along York Hill Boulevard in the first leg of my journey. There was a light snow falling in the crisp January night. I peered out the rear-view mirror every five seconds and drove well below the speed limit.

Twenty minutes later I arrived at the Sheraton Parkway where I motored to a distant spot in the parking lot. I inched toward the entrance, alert to the danger of Leah's presence in every direction.

Before I pushed through the revolving doors at the front of the building I glanced behind me once last time.

That's when I bumped into him.

Jake!

I drew back and tried to avert my face.

"Sorry," he said. He stepped away and stared at me.

Why was he still there? Was he trying to torture her? I pushed into the glass doors with clammy hands as fast as the revolving door would take me.

With Jake apparently off my tail I surveyed the lobby until my eyes alighted on the back of Leah sitting on a couch. Her head was in her hands and her shoulders shook violently.

My urge to rush over to her battled with the necessity of escaping her line of vision. My heart raced as I considered how visible I was, stationed next to the front desk. Leah suddenly raised her head to pull a tissue from her Zara bag, then dabbed at her eyes. The muscles in my legs tightened. I had to will them not to start running because those legs were pretty darned determined to get out of Dodge.

When she was done, she rested her forehead in her hand, giving me the opportunity to slink toward the bathroom. I tiptoed across the marble floor to the safety of the bathroom where I examined the long row of wooden doors. I hurried to the last stall and opened the door. I found a frosted glass shelf attached to the rear wall with a silk plant glued on top. I tugged the envelope from my purse and gently wedged it between the plant and the tile.

My bangs were sealed to my forehead with an adhesive of fear. I exited the bathroom and sidled through the lobby as far away from the couch as possible. Leah was still sobbing silently. I swallowed and raced out of the lobby into the black night. Where the snow had turned into rain. Once inside Leah's car I exhaled slowly to calm my racing heart. When my hands stopped shaking I dispatched an email to Leah with instructions for finding the cash.

I powered out of the lot with the rain heavy now. The rhythmic motion of the wipers throbbed like an infected tooth. A fresh swell of sadness rose in me as I visualized Leah alone in the corner of the hotel lobby, weeping silently.

As I approached Yonge Street my phone rang.

"Rain! Is everything alright?" It was Professor K. "I've been worried about you. You were supposed to be here two hours ago."

chapter 25

I slapped my hand on my head; I had completely forgotten that I was supposed to go pick up the Faulkner essay that he had offered to edit. At this point it was going to be a miracle if I passed half of my courses this semester, so his help was crucial. I felt terrible about Professor K. He'd even postponed a date with Esther so he could meet me. I glanced at the clock on the dash. It was 9:45 p.m. Bubby would be asleep by now and Mira and Eli weren't coming back from Stratford until the next day. "I'll swing by, Professor K.," I said. "I'm really sorry about this."

"I look forward to it."

I hung a right onto New Westminster Drive. With the rain

drumming on the roof, the car sounded like the inside of a tin can. When I arrived at his house thirty minutes later, we bypassed the pureed vegetables and headed straight to the computer. I pulled up a chair as Professor K. opened Word to find my paper on William Faulkner.

"First of all," he said. "I want to congratulate you on a well-written paper."

"You do?"

My phone attempted to interrupt us but I ignored the ringing. When the call repeated two more times Professor K. told me to answer.

"Rain, it's me, Deb."

"I'm kind of busy now," I said. Professor K. flipped through the printout of my essay.

"I just want you to know that I've made peace with Brutus. We're okay now."

"Excellent, you fed the dog a treat?"

"Better. I went to Walmart and got him a big bag of choco-late. Choco-chickies were on sale."

"Who wouldn't love chocolate?"

Professor K.'s eyes widened under his thick frames.

"Oh yeah," she said. "And considering how oversized he is, I got him sugar-free chocolate. The only thing worse than a Great Dane is a fat Great Dane. Anyway when I left Daniel's apartment he was licking my hand."

"They should package sugar-free chocolate treats for big dogs."

Professor K. shook his head back and forth. I was starting to get a bit rattled.

"Hang on," I said to Deb. I turned to Professor K. "Are you okay?"

His brows knit with worry. "Chocolate is toxic for dogs. It affects their hearts and nervous systems. We *never* gave Chaucer chocolate."

Uh-oh.

"Sugar substitutes are especially dangerous for dogs," he said. "They can lead to coma or even death."

A ball of nausea started bouncing in my belly.

"Oh my god, I heard that!" Deb said on the other end of the line. "Daniel will hate me."

She had a point.

"I shouldn't have been cheap," she said, her voice trembling. "I should have just bought him a pie."

"It was the principle."

"Darn right."

Professor K. tapped on the desk. "Rain, the dog might be fine but your friend really should take the dog to the vet *immediately*."

"My car's in for repairs. How am I going to get him to a vet?" Deb was practically sobbing now.

"Can't you just take a cab?"

"Have you seen the weather out there? The rain's turned to snow. It's a mess. It'll be an hour wait."

No, no, no, no. Don't ask.

"Rain, would you mind terribly driving me and Bronx to the vet? I'll walk over to Daniel's place and meet you there."

I glanced at my watch. Dahlia would still be at the bar mitzvah so she wasn't available. Since I had created this situation, I needed to own it.

"Okay," I said. "Tell me where he lives, then call the vet."

As I flew out the door, Professor K. called after me, "Try to give the dog some water! And let me know how it goes!"

I punched Daniel's address into my GPS, put the car in gear and raced down Bathurst Street. I floored the pedal and the car careened through the intersection, my hands curled so tightly around the steering wheel that it felt like it would snap off the dashboard any second.

When I arrived at Daniel's side split bungalow, I bolted up the front steps and flew through the front door. My stomach dropped when I found Bronx lying at the foot of the sink, the empty box of Choco-chickies next to him. Deb was kneeling on the floor and gently stroking his back.

I dropped to the floor. "Bronx," I whispered. "Are you okay?"

As if in answer, he raised his head and his eyes fluttered for a second. My heart skipped a beat.

"Come on, big guy," Deb said with a quivering voice. Bronx turned to Deb and his eyes locked on hers. You could see the bulb going off in his brain — it was the moment of truth. The hyper-intuitive animal; the amateur therapist. It was an "aha" moment as he confronted the agent of his harm.

Bronx's mouth gaped wide open. Deb and I eyed each other with terror as he leaned over to her with his jaw hanging open.

And licked her face.

She exhaled, hugged him, then jumped up and raised her arms. "Thank god. He lives, he lives, he lives. The dog lives!"

I rose to my feet and wiped off some stray dog hairs from my skirt. Bronx watched Deb with a goofy look, almost a smile, and then promptly collapsed onto the floor again. We gasped in horror as his eyelids slowly closed.

"Oh my god! Oh my god!" Deb was screaming. Or I was screaming. I'm still not sure.

"The vet!" I said, as I sank to the floor again and stroked Bronx on his back. "Please, Bronx. Can you please get up?"

Bronx lifted his head again and slurped my face, like it was covered with pie. Or kibble. "How are we going to get him into the car?" I said. He was the size of a motorcycle, and seemed to be too woozy to do anything more than shower us with slimy affection.

"Okay, so you take the front, I'll take the back," she said. I grasped his shoulder and Deb pulled his legs and we yanked, but Bronx was too heavy to lift. I grabbed Bronx's collar with both of my hands and tugged. He slid around three inches across the ceramic tiles with an amused look on his face. I think he was actually enjoying the attention.

"Think, think, think," she said, placing her hand on her head.

"When's Daniel coming back?" I said. I cringed as Bronx licked my face again.

"Tomorrow afternoon. He's flying back from Philadelphia."

"That's it!" I shouted. "Let's get a suitcase with wheels. Does he have more than one?"

"Brilliant! I'll go look." Deb's eyes darted around the room as she tore out of the kitchen. She pounded through the living room and stomped down the stairs, the force rattling the crystal lighting fixture in the dining room. I scooped up Bronx's bowl and poured in a bottle of water from Daniel's pantry, then placed it in front of him. He took a few sips and then smiled at me.

Deb charged into the kitchen pulling an enormous black moulded plastic suitcase the size of a phone booth. She placed it on the floor next to Bronx and ripped open the zipper.

"Okay," she said as she propped up the suitcase on its side.

"All we need to do is pick him up just enough to tip him into the suitcase. Then we roll him out to the car."

This was an excellent plan. "I take the front, you take the bottom," I said. "Let's count to three and pick him up."

"One, two, three, *push!*" We dragged his forelegs over the side of the suitcase and on the second shove deposited the rest of his body inside. We tipped the suitcase upright and Bronx fell right in. I zipped up both sides, leaving the top open for air. Deb extended the plastic handle and gingerly pulled the suitcase toward the front door.

I bolted into the living room and yanked a folded fleece blanket from the end of the couch and then tripped out the front door of the house.

I was glad that it was dark outside. I didn't want any neighbours taking this the wrong way, like we were carting a body out to the car or something. We were, but you know what I mean.

I helped Deb gently ease the suitcase down the three stairs and then we pulled it up to the backseat of the Saturn. I threw the blanket over the back then we hoisted the suitcase and gently tipped it over, rolling Bronx onto the backseat.

Deb stroked his face one more time. "I'm so sorry, Big Guy," she said in a whisper. "You're going to be okay, alright?" He answered her with another face lick with his enormous tongue. As a bonus he raised his paw and stroked her arm. I had to admit, as a non-dog person, Bronx was kind of growing on me.

She squeezed his paw, and then hurtled back into Daniel's house, dragging the empty suitcase behind her and locked his door. Deb bolted back to the Saturn and jumped into the passenger seat, panting. I put the car in reverse and rocketed out of the driveway onto the empty street.

"Watch the speed bumps!" Deb roared. She turned around, leaned over to the backseat, and stroked Bronx's ear. "I just wanted him to be my friend," she said in a tearful voice. "I should have researched dogs more. It's all my fault."

No, it wasn't *all* her fault. I mean the chocolate part was, but it was my idea to win over Bronx. It was nothing short of miraculous that Professor K. heard my conversation with Deb and told me to take the dog to the vet.

Deb pulled out her cell phone, keyed in a number, and babbled.

"Daniel, it's me, Deb. I feel sick to my stomach but I made a huge mistake and left some treats for . . . Bronx . . . and didn't know that chocolate was dangerous."

She paused briefly and stifled a sob. "I'm on my way to the vet with him now and I'll stay with him all night. I'm so sorry. If you hate me for this I understand. I feel like a horrible person. Daniel, please forgive me."

She closed her phone and wiped her eye with the back of her hand. I reached out and squeezed her shoulder. She leaned over to the dashboard and jabbed the radio button, flipping between stations.

"What are you doing?" I said, as a jumble of sounds stabbed the air and assaulted my ears.

"Bronx loves jazz," Deb said as she frantically punched the scan button. She finally settled on a station, cranked up the volume, and a forty-piece 1950s band convulsed the car. She squeezed her eyes shut, tears rolling down her cheeks. "This is all so wrong."

I glanced at her. "Deb, he's going to be okay —"

"You don't get it," she said, her head snapping toward me. "This is swing. *He needs Miles Davis.*"

"I completely agree."

Deb peered behind her at the rear seat. "His eyes are closed again!" she yelled. *"Drive faster!"*

I gunned the car, just missing an ancient Chevy driven by nothing more than two bony hands grasping the steering wheel. I could have kicked myself for my stupid idea.

"Faster!" Deb said.

I lurched to the right lane but within seconds a tiny Smart Car emerged from a parking spot. We veered back into the left lane, rocking violently like we were on a sideways roller coaster.

"Actually, your driving is kind of making me sick," Deb said in a quiet voice.

And then I smelled it. I looked out the window at the bungalows that lined the neat street but there were no signs of farms anywhere close by. I opened my window.

"Do you smell that?" I asked. I jammed the radio button off. The car seemed suddenly bigger, emptied of all that dance music.

"Um, Rain? I'm . . . really sorry."

"Oh. Is that you?"

"Um, no," Deb said in a tiny voice. "It's kind of . . . dog vomit."

"Dog vomit?! Dog vomit?!" I yelled at Deb.

"I think your driving made Bronx carsick."

I twisted around and glanced behind me. A sticky patch of dog vomit flecked with chunks of Choco-chickies lay under his matted head and dripped off the seat, forming a sickening puddle in the foot well. I could feel my eyes filling up. Deb rested her hand lightly on my shoulder. "Maybe the vomit is good because the chocolate is coming out."

That vomit might have been good for Bronx. And it might have been good for Deb. But it was very, very bad for my sister's car, which meant that it was very, very bad for me. I glanced in the rear-view mirror. Bronx was trying to rise on his forelegs. He looked around him and then sank back into his seat, his eyes closed again.

I thought of the Post-it notes in my desk. This is the list I would have made.

     People Who Have Totally Legitimate Reasons to Hate Me:
     #1. Daniel: Because I killed his dog.
     #2. Leah: Because I killed her car.
     #3. Bronx: Because I killed him.

And as a freebie I'd throw in Mrs. Levine just because she hated me already.

"I'll figure out a way to clean out the car," Deb said.

"My sister . . . ," I stuttered. "I have to pick her up —"

"We'll get rid of this stuff and the smell," she said.

"— in the morning."

"Yeah, that might be a problem," she said. "It's here!" She pointed to the small bungalow with a large sandblasted sign that said Emergency Animal Clinic. I lurched into the drive-way. Deb threw open her door and sprinted toward the house. I peered back at Bronx who was trying to rise to his feet again. That was definitely an improvement. Deb emerged from the animal clinic with a burly man pulling a gurney. He removed a wooden board with black straps dangling from the sides from the stretcher.

"OdoBan," the man said while he manoeuvred the board

under Bronx. "You can get it at any Home Store — it gets out bad dog smells."

The man buckled Bronx down on both sides of the wooden board. He and Deb eased the board from the car onto the gurney then pulled it toward the clinic.

"Are you sure you don't need me to help?" Deb called behind her.

"Your place is with Bronx now," I said. "Go to him now. He needs you." It was like a scene from a cheesy movie where you'd expect to hear the swelling of violins in the background as the heroine ran in slow motion to her beloved. Except we were dealing with a barfing dog, a putrid car, and a whole lot of people who were going to be pretty ticked off by the time this incident was over.

Deb nodded tearfully at me and mouthed thank-you-I'm-so-sorry as I backed the Saturn out of the driveway.

I drove to the twenty-four-hour Home Store where I purchased the animal cleaner, then rushed home. I found a plastic bucket but no rags anywhere in the laundry room so I ran upstairs to my bedroom, grabbed the only thing I could find — my favourite night T-shirt — and ripped it into large pieces. I filled the bucket with warm water and spent the next couple of hours in the frozen night, scrubbing vomit, scouring the upholstery, and wiping all the plastic parts in Leah's car.

At 3:30 a.m. I opened the windows to air out, prayed it wouldn't rain or snow any more that night, and dragged myself up to my bedroom and crashed fully clothed into my bed.

chapter 26
Disaster DNA

At 6 a.m. I was awoken by my cell phone shrieking in my ear.

"Rain, it's me," Leah said.

"You okay?" I said.

"My shift is over and I'm at Finch Station and I'm really, really tired," she said. "Can you pick me up?"

I bolted upright. "I'd be happy to, but the only car here is yours."

"I'm not doing well and I'm desperate. Can you just drive really, really carefully? The keys are in a ceramic bowl on my desk."

"I'll be right there."

I threw on a stretchy skirt and a sweatshirt, grabbed her

keys, and slid into the driver's seat of Leah's car. I glanced behind me. There was no sign of dog sickness and there was a pleasant scent in the air. It still made sense to drive with the windows down to be on the safe side though.

I pulled into the station where Leah waited. Her eyes were blotchy and her face was puffy from crying. The Zara bag carried the remains of her last night's disastrous date. She walked over to the driver's seat and threw in her purse. I climbed over the console and settled into the passenger seat while she threw the Zara bag in the trunk.

She lowered herself into the driver seat and let out a yelp. "Why does my car smell like . . . like . . . What *is* this?"

What was with the x-ray smelling abilities? I shrunk back in my seat and answered in a quivering voice. "Vomit."

"Vomit?!" she yelled. "Did you use my car?"

I shrunk back toward the passenger window. How could I possibly explain this? "It's a long story —"

She whipped up her hand to stop me.

"Please don't say anything. I can't handle your excuses now."

She keyed the ignition and pulled a sharp left onto Yonge Street. Forget gas, the car was running on anger now. A horrible, terrible, frightening silence filled the car like a balloon about to explode. I gripped the armrest, terrified to look at her now.

Yonge Street was like an empty runway and the car was about to fly off the ground.

She didn't say a word until we pulled into the Bernsteins' house where for some reason Uncle Eli's car was parked on the driveway. Leah sprung from the seat, unlatched the trunk, grabbed the Zara bag and slammed down the hatch, the car rocking back and forth from the force.

When we got into the house, Mira was carting her suitcase up the stairs.

"Girls!" she said. "We decided to come home early and beat the traffic back from Stratford. How are you?"

Leah threw her bag on the floor and took a deep breath. "Do you want to know what happened? Rain took my car *without permission* and threw up in it."

Aunt Mira slowly descended the stairs. "Rain? Are you alright?"

"It's a long story," I said.

"You had no permission," Leah said. She exhaled through clenched teeth then turned to Aunt Mira. "I can't take it anymore, Aunt Mira."

"It," meaning me.

This was clearly part of a larger conversation that she and Mira were carrying on about me. My shoulders crumpled.

"I don't know *what's* going on with her," Leah said.

"What *is* going on, Rain?" Mira said. "Now."

Leah glared at me with narrowed eyes. You could practically see the gears turning in her head and when she spoke it was barely a whisper. "You were there."

I shook my head. This couldn't be happening.

"You *stalked me on my date* last night."

I gasped.

She turned to Aunt Mira. "The jerk I was dating —" Leah stopped and shuddered. She squeezed her eyes shut and wiped them with her fingers. "He dumped me last night, but he came back to check on me, and told me that my sister was lurking at the Sheraton, but I didn't believe him."

My mouth dropped.

"I thought I saw my car pull into the parking lot," Leah said to me. Her face looked like it had been punched with betrayal. "So you *followed* me? I thought you were starting to grow up."

"There's a reason," I sobbed. "I can explain."

"She's probably reading my emails," Leah said to Mira. "She's sneaking around at night. She looked like she might have been drinking at Jeremy's engagement party. Who knows what she's up to?"

Her eyes squeezed shut as a fresh batch of tears formed. "Aunt Mira, I'm so tired. I need to sleep now. I'll talk to you later," she said as she climbed the stairs.

"Rain," Mira said in a quiet voice. "I've already spoken to your parents. We'll have to reassess whether this year's plan is working."

I shuddered and wiped my eye with the back of my hand.

"Go get your lunch. I'll take you to the bus stop in ten minutes," she said.

Who cared about food? I gathered my knapsack and stumbled to the foyer where I slumped on the deacon's bench. The last twelve hours had been a complete nightmare. I had a car disaster, a sister disaster, a dog disaster, and possibly a Bernstein disaster. I had disaster DNA imprinted on every cell in my body.

Exhaustion overcame me. If only I could just drift into a dreamy sleep, then wake to find that all my problems had been fixed. I leaned back against the wall and closed my eyes, but the disturbing picture of Bronx jabbed my head. I possibly poisoned him and then made him carsick. With growing dread I pulled my cell phone from my purse.

There were no messages or texts from Deb.

I signed into Matchmaven.

There were two emails in the inbox. The first was a letter from Daniel. I bit my lip and slowly clicked on his message.

> Dear Matchmaven,
>
> Thank you so much for all your help last night. I've been in touch with Deb for the last few hours and Bronx is fine! Deb was beside herself with concern but she actually saved him! I'm so impressed with her efforts and her dedication. I think this is the sign I was looking for. She's our hero. Don't say anything, but she's definitely The One!
> Best,
> Daniel

Thank. You. God.

Bronx was okay. And Deb and Daniel too. I felt a drop of relief, which was not quite as much fun as happiness, but I took it anyway.

And then a seed of hope began to blossom. If Bronx could rise from the dead, then anything could happen. That dog was a beacon of hope: a shining light in the abyss of my life. Bronx was the 2004 Red Sox coming back from a three-game deficit to triumph over the Yankees. Bronx was the brave men who swept the Cardinals and won the World Series, finally ending the Curse of the Bambino once and for all.

Maybe it was exhaustion or possibly desperation, or maybe it was even insanity, but my mind brimmed with Bronx. For me he was optimism, promise, and redemption, all wrapped in one massive beast.

I was high on a shot of Bronx.

"We'll leave in five minutes," Mira yelled down from upstairs.

"Okay, I'm ready whenever you are," I shouted back.

The second email was from Tamara.

> Hi Rain,
>
> I miss you! I'm so sorry that I've disappeared into my wedding. Please can we get together next week? You name the night and I'll be available. Maybe we'll meet after school and I'll take you out to dinner.
>
> I still feel bad about Matchmaven, but it sounds like you're doing an amazing job.
>
> Hugs,
>
> Tamara

A smile lit up my face. I hadn't realized how much I missed Tamara while she was gone.

It was the postscript that made me freeze.

> P.S. Remember I told you about my friend Aviva? She was temporarily working as a secretary at your old high school and the position of chemistry teacher just opened up so she got the job! Isn't that great? Apparently the previous teacher, (Mr. Sacks — did you know him?) had a heart attack and is in a Manhattan ICU now.

chapter 27
Unwelcome Images

My chin and lips trembled uncontrollably and my body went cold as I followed Mira out the front door, staggered down the icy stairs, and stumbled into her Camry.

I turned away from Mira and leaned against the window. "You have a sniffle, are you okay?" Mira said, handing me a tissue.

I battled to control my voice. "I think I'm coming down with something. I just need a good night's sleep." By the time I got to school I felt like I had drill bits boring into my brain.

Mr. Sacks was in the hospital.

I felt nauseated.

Let's see: I go into the computer lab. I sit down at a computer last June. I discover that his browser is still open. I send off humiliating emails from his account poking fun at him and his memory. Two weeks later, he gets notice. Two months later, he's replaced. Five months later, he has a heart attack. You do the math.

I plodded to Jewish History class blinking back tears.

I had to apologize before it was too late. I simply could not spend the rest of my life like Esther. I had no choice. The New York bar mitzvah might be my last chance to apologize to him.

When I got to class I threw down my knapsack on the desk next to Dahlia. She rose from her seat when she saw my blotchy face.

"What's wrong?" she said. "I don't feel well so I'm going home."

"No! You can't leave."

"Sorry," she said with a pained expression. "I kind of have a . . . Lillian Shimmel thing. You okay?"

I shook my head and fell into the seat. "That teacher, Mr. Sacks? He had a massive heart attack."

"Oh no!" Dahlia said. The only thing preventing me from throwing myself in the snow were two magical words.

New. York.

Dahlia clenched her teeth, then rose and threw her pencil case into her knapsack. "Do you think he got your letter?"

"I don't know." I shook my head. "All I know is that I need to find his hospital and apologize to him personally."

She zipped up her knapsack. "I'm so sorry."

"Go home and get better," I said. I opened my notebook, and mindlessly wrote words, fixing my gaze on one of those tiny, inexplicable apple stickers that was stuck to the desk. Unwelcome images violated my mind.

Like sitting in the waiting room with my parents, before we met with Rabbi Singer.

The staff at Maimonides murmuring things about me.

My mother's stricken face as Rabbi Singer told us that it would be better if I chose another school. Every hair on my head, every cell in my body, and every square inch of me was ablaze with shame.

There was only one hope of redeeming myself now.

New York. New York. New York. It was a chant that played over in my head, like a prayer.

At lunchtime, I ducked outside the school. Dahlia had gone home so I was truly alone. Slumped alone next to the rusting Dumpster, I was able to focus on attaining flawless hysteria. The image of Mr. Sacks lying in a hospital bed with a broken heart hit my internal refresh button every few minutes, setting off a new surge of fear. The biting wind curled around my body like a serpent and tightened me in its grip.

All I had was the flame of hope. I was going to apologize to Mr. Sacks and really, really mean it.

New York. New York. New York.

At the beginning of English class I handed in my paper. Professor K. liked me — because he didn't know me. Like Tamara. Like everyone.

The next morning Mira and I set out to the bus, except that she motored past the Number 7 bus stop.

"Aunt Mira," I said. "You missed my stop."

"Oh sweetie, I'm taking you down to school today."

"What about work?"

"We're going to have a little meeting at school first."

A little meeting? That could mean only one thing — a big meeting. If she was driving me down to school and getting into work late, I was obviously facing a big, horrible, life-altering meeting.

We pulled into the school parking lot and I stumbled out of the car across the icy pavement. Could anything make my life worse now? Why, yes it could. When we got to Mrs. Levine's office, Mrs. Marmor was sitting there too.

"Why don't you both sit down?" Mrs. Levine said to my aunt and me. "I trust you're doing well?" Mrs. Levine said to me. I didn't bother irritating her with a response.

I glanced at Mrs. Marmor hoping for an indication of where this was going. She gave me one of her signature knit-eyebrow smiles. You know, the kind that lets you know that she can feel the tragedy of your very existence.

The three women all nodded at each other, like everything had been choreographed.

Mrs. Levine was the first to speak. "Raina, the reason that we're all here today is because we share tremendous concerns about your situation right now."

I blinked.

"You seem to be struggling in most of your classes and we're concerned that there are deeper issues at the core of your situation."

"I'm really sorry, Raina," Mrs. Marmor said quietly. "But I'm going to ask you a very difficult question and we would all appreciate a completely honest answer."

My heart seized for a moment. Did I leave Matchmaven open on the computer? No one really ever used that old computer in the den. My aunt and uncle owned their own laptops and Leah had gotten one too. So even if I did leave it open, who would have seen it?

Mrs. Marmor leaned over and peered at me with a grave

expression. "I don't know if there's a delicate way to ask this."

My stomach clenched. "What is it?"

"Rain, are you on drugs?"

"What?" I almost jumped out of my seat. "No! Of course not!"

It was Aunt Mira's turn now. "Rain, we're just trying to help you. Are you using alcohol?"

"Aunt Mira, how could you even ask me that?"

"We're all very concerned about you. It's almost like you have . . . I don't know how to put my finger on it. Some sort of double life. Is something going on with you?"

"*Nothing* is going on." I crossed my arms. "Nothing at all."

Mrs. Marmor leaned over with her nauseatingly good cop voice. "Rain, this is a safe environment and if you need it we can get you help."

"I promise you I'm not doing drugs or alcohol."

They all exchanged knowing glances at each other as they prepared to move into the second act.

"Rain, I called Mrs. Levine to let her know that you were going to New York for the bar mitzvah," Mira said.

I held my breath.

Mrs. Levine clasped her hands together on her desk. "You know that the student rule book says you can't miss school or take any trips without prior permission of the school," Mrs. Levine said of her beloved student rule book. "So when your aunt called to ask permission I had to be frank with her. You're failing too many classes. I've spoken to you about it a number of times, but it's only getting worse."

My body seized into one huge muscle spasm. "Sorry?"

"I'm really sorry, Raina. I've discussed it with your mother," Aunt Mira said. "The trip is too close to exams and you're in danger of failing too many of your classes. You'd have to miss two school days. It's too risky."

I bolted out of my chair. "You can't *do* that."

"Rain," she hissed at me, peering at Mrs. Levine out of the corner of her eye. "Sit down."

"Rain," Mrs. Marmor said in her Soothing Voice. "Try to relax."

"Please sit down, Raina," Mrs. Levine said.

I dropped back into my chair. "I've been *living* for that. I'll do anything you tell me, please."

"I'm really sorry, sweetie," Mira said. "I'm happy to get you some extra tutoring until exams. If you work hard —"

I shook my head back and forth. "I just need some time. Just give me a chance to catch up." I could only hope that she'd finish up before I threw up.

"Despite all the support that the school is offering you, your academic situation is deteriorating rapidly," Mrs. Levine said quietly. "On the surface, it doesn't look like your move to Toronto is really benefitting you."

My heart beat furiously. Was she kicking me out? "But it's still early in the year —"

She raised her hands upright.

"It's not so early — we're a week away from the end of the semester. I'm not saying you have to leave. Not yet, anyway. But your situation is very, very precarious. I'm looking at the rest of this year, and the implications for the next one. If your marks don't rally and go through a dramatic improvement between now and the end of the semester exams, we'll need to reassess the situation."

I gasped. I couldn't get kicked out. I had nowhere to go. And I could *not* live in my parents' living room in Hong Kong.

"Raina," Mrs. Marmor leaned over and spoke sympathetically. "You have ten days until exams to turn things around. You're an intelligent girl. I know that you actually scored high in your entrance exam to Maimonides."

"Look, I can *easily* pass my courses," I said. "I can throw myself into studying."

"Exactly why you need to stay here," Mrs. Levine said. "Your aunt wasn't sure about what to do about your trip and I had to be honest with my opinion."

"Please, no," I moaned.

"I'm sorry, Raina," Mrs. Levine said. "It's just not worth trading away your entire academic year for one long weekend in New York."

How on earth was I going to apologize to Mr. Sacks? *The man could be dying now.*

It felt like the entire insides of my body were lined with lighter fluid. I was completely flammable now. If I looked at Mrs. Levine's hateful face for a moment longer I would ignite. I stared at the mottled floor tiles and tried to calm my crazed pulse.

And if I combusted, the first thing I was going to take down with me was that detestable woman.

chapter 28

→→→ We Feel Your Pain, Blah, Blah, Blah ←←←

I struggled to regain my breath. I wondered: Was this how Mr. Sacks felt about me? And Leah too? The secretary, Mrs. Abrams, knocked on the door and leaned her head in the office. "Mrs. Levine. Can I speak to you for a minute?"

Mrs. Levine rose from her seat. "I'll be right back. Mrs. Bernstein, is there anything else you wanted to discuss?"

"No, Mrs. Levine," she said, and then turned to me. "It'll be okay," she said in a whisper. They both left the office.

"Rain," Mrs. Marmor said in a soft voice. "I'm here for you if you want to talk."

"Do you want me to share my *feelings*?" I snarled.

She raised her hands and nodded. "Only if you want to. I

221

can imagine how upsetting this must be."

"Upsetting?" I spat out. I stared at the ridiculous picture of Mrs. Levine with her two young grandsons. Did they have any idea of what a truly hideous woman their grandmother was?

"I have to go to New York."

"Of course you do. But I've got to be honest." She picked up the RESNICK, RAINA file and rifled through a number of papers. "Your uncle tutors you, you're not in any clubs, and you're not involved with any extracurricular activities. You're a month away from the end of the semester and you're now failing history, English, math, and possibly anthropology. Your highest mark is in phys. ed and that's only 63 percent. The gym teacher says you're listless all the time."

Mrs. Marmor returned the papers to the file and set it on the table and then looked up at me. "Is something going on?"

"I have to go to New York."

She leaned over and placed her hand over mine. "I'm not sure that it's worth throwing out the rest of high school for a weekend in New York. Why is this so important?"

I took in a deep breath and exhaled slowly. "I need to find Mr. Sacks."

"Oh, I see," she said, leaning back in her chair and squeezing her lips together like she was spreading the lip gloss. She nodded slowly. "Why now?"

"It's just, the last few weeks . . . ," I said, trying to slow my breathing. "I've tried writing him."

She studied me as if she was recalibrating me.

"You wrote Mr. Sacks?"

"Yes. A few times."

She peered at me and her face softened into a smile. "Wow. You really should feel very proud of yourself." I waited.

"I feel terrible saying this," Mrs. Marmor said. "But it won't sway Mrs. Levine. I think you'll have to wait until spring break or summer vacation to see him. I'm so sorry."

"Please," I said, running my fingers through my bangs. "He's ill. Can't you try talking to her?"

She shook her head. "She's made up her mind," she said, rising from her seat.

And clearly, so had Mrs. Marmor. I wanted to scream, just *do* something.

"Rain," she said. "You should let this go and focus on fixing things in the next few weeks. You know that my door is always open if you need me."

We feel your pain, but there's nothing we can do, blah, blah, blah.

She got up and left the office. Alone in Mrs. Levine's lair and visually assaulted by signs of her existence, I felt yet another tidal wave of hatred wash over me. I stood up to distract myself from the burning tears that were threatening to spew. I stared at that old picture of Mrs. Levine and her husband that hung on the wall behind her chair. The one where she had the huge hair — and I mean gigantic hair. His arm was draped across her shoulder and he lovingly leaned into her. Mrs. Levine's head was tilted up to him, her eyes crinkled in a smile, with a look of wonder on her face. It was a side to Mrs. Levine that I'd never actually experienced. You know — the human one.

The outfit was Mrs. Levine Classic. In fact, I recognized her green dress. It was the same outfit that she wore when I met her in her office last Thursday. Mrs. Levine wore a necklace that prominently hung from her turtleneck. I inched over behind her desk and studied the photograph.

It was an unusual necklace; the pendant was gold and seemed to be shaped like an animal. I leaned in and squinted at the necklace and felt the hairs on the back of my neck prickling. No. It couldn't be.

It was an elephant.

There were three rubies on the gold elephant.

Impossible. This was impossible.

There were four Hebrew letters engraved in the gold. Hebrew for Esther.

Blood rushed like rapids through my body as the reality of the situation flooded me.

Mrs. Levine *was Esther. Matchmaven's Esther.*

chapter 29

→ Playing with Matches ←

My feet froze like they were sealed inside two buckets of concrete.

No. No. It couldn't be.

If Mrs. Levine was Esther, then who were these children and grandchildren? Esther hadn't remarried, and she definitely never had kids. I scanned Mrs. Levine's sparse office, but there was nothing to indicate her first name anywhere. There were no diplomas or awards on her desk or walls. A pile of papers nestled in a metal tray. I glanced up at the doorway. Mrs. Abrams, the secretary, was chatting on the phone and the reception area was empty. I inched toward the tray, blocking the line of sight to the outer office with my body.

The letter on top of the tray was from a board member, but wasn't addressed with her first name. I rifled through the papers underneath, but couldn't find anything there either.

I stepped back from behind the desk just as Mrs. Abrams poked her head in the office again.

"Rain, Mrs. Levine has a school emergency. There are some broken pipes in the boiler room. She said to let you know that you can leave now."

"Thank you," I mumbled. Mrs. Abrams turned to leave.

"Mrs. Abrams?" I asked in a halting voice, pointing to the cluster of family photos on Mrs. Levine's desk. "Are these . . . are these her grandkids?"

"No," she said, shaking her head sadly. "They're her sister's children and grandchildren. Beautiful, aren't they?" She turned back to the reception area.

I nodded, my mouth hanging open. I stole across the room to the bookshelf, and furtively pulled out a worn Hebrew prayer book, opened it with shaking hands, and read the bookplate.

This book belongs to Esther Levine.

I snapped it shut and returned it to the shelf, my heart pounding so hard it had to be scarring my insides.

It was too much to absorb. As much as Mrs. Levine and I disliked each other, our alter egos had completely connected. Actually both my secret identity and I liked Esther, and Esther and Mrs. Levine liked Matchmaven. It was just Rain and Mrs. Levine who couldn't stand each other. It was too complicated. We weren't just two people anymore. We were like a complicated clique of girls.

I needed a vomitorium.

I fled the office. All day I scurried between classes

petrified of running into Mrs. Levine in the halls. I felt like I was sealed in a Ziploc baggie of silence, oblivious to everything going on around me. My internal volcano spewed a cascade of emotions and thoughts that alternated between terror and confusion. Deb and Ilana had figured out who I was. What if Mrs. Levine discovered Matchmaven's real identity? She'd be humiliated — and furious that she had confided in me.

When I opened my inbox that night, of course there was another lovely email from Esther. That would be Esther the elegant. Esther the intelligent. Esther the soft-spoken friend. But Mrs. Levine, the cold and heartless? How could they be the same person?

It was like mixing equal parts nail polish and nail polish remover.

It had never occurred to me that fixing people up was like playing with matches. Running away was looking like a mighty fine option right now.

I needed an island.

Quickly.

> Dear Matchmaven,
>
> I hope you're doing well. Thank you for the advice about a present for Mo. Meeting him has been a gift. I know you're overwhelmed, but hold on. Good things happen in the end. I hope that work issue resolves itself for you soon. I have some challenging issues at work too, but I'm so much more optimistic about everything! There were some facility problems today. And I've got a lovely young individual who has tremendous potential but is somewhat self-destructive. She has such a lovely spirit, though. I know

that everyone has to make their own mistakes, but it's

hard to watch. I guess it all comes back to second chances.

And I'm grateful you gave me one.

Best regards,

Esther

I thought of the previous email I had sent to her referring to problems she was giving me. I had complained about Mrs. Levine to Mrs. Levine.

I had no idea how to talk to her anymore. Especially because the discussion was veering toward an awkward topic: me. It's not like I was going to argue with her about me not *really* being self-destructive. That was the thing about Matchmaven. Except for the fact that it was all falling apart, it was actually a fantastic surveillance system that fed me information that I never would have learned otherwise.

Leah and Mrs. Levine had told Matchmaven insights about me that I couldn't have learned, because people just don't say these things to your face.

Even when your face needs it.

It was pretty amazing to realize that living a double life could actually lead you to the truth about yourself. But the problem is that as awesome as it can be for your emotional growth, it's not so great for your relationships. In some ways, the secrecy in my life was my friend; it allowed me to connect with Leah and with Esther and gave me the ability to try to help them and other people.

But all the good things were making me look very bad. Thanks to Matchmaven, Leah and Mrs. Levine had a low opinion of me, and who could blame them? Because of Matchmaven's activities, Leah thought I was stalking her and getting into trouble, and Mrs. Levine thought I was just blow-ing off my studies and didn't care about school.

I did nothing all evening but compose draft after draft until 11:30, when I finished the email and hit the send button.

> Dear Esther,
>
> I'm delighted that things are going so well with you and Mo.
>
> > I think sometimes when we suffer regret for our actions it's hard to watch a younger person make similar mistakes. Maybe this individual just needs to go through her own learning process and that'll be a thousand times more valuable than any lecture or advice.
>
> Warm regards,
>
> MM

I pulled out the Post-it notes from my drawer and made a new list.

> *Bad Things that Are Happening to Me:*
> #1. Leah hates me — it's permanent now.
> #2. Mrs. Levine still hates me.
> #3. I'm about to get kicked out of school again.
> #4. Mr. Sacks might be dying.
> #5. Mrs. Levine IS ESTHER !?!?!?!?

Oy.

chapter 30

>>>> → Dragon Lady ← ⋘

Everything was so broken now. Especially me.

At this point Leah and I avoided each other like we would a communicable disease. Dahlia was still home with the flu so I was completely on my own.

I was still hoping that Leah would at least contact Match-maven, so I kept popping into the bathroom all morning to check my email. At lunchtime I passed Shira, Natalie, and Sarah chatting in the hallway just as Mrs. Levine walked by.

"Raina!"

I did a double take. The colour was obviously all wrong, *but Mrs. Levine was wearing lipstick!*

"How are your exam preparations coming along?" she said.

Earrings too!

"They're okay. I'm trying."

"Oh really?" She smiled slightly.

I repeat. Mrs. Levine smiled at me. I thought about her most recent email.

I've got a lovely young individual who has tremendous potential . . .

"I hope you'll be focused, Raina. There's not much time left."

"Thanks, Mrs. Levine," I said quietly. Natalie snorted.

I trudged to the bathroom more confused than ever. How was I supposed to make amends with Mr. Sacks? And what was I supposed to do about Mrs. Levine? If she found out I was Matchmaven, it would definitely get back to Mira — then Leah. I sat on the covered toilet and pulled out my phone from my pocket just as a group of familiar voices entered the bathroom.

"Shira, you should have seen Dragon Lady on her way out," a voice that sounded like Natalie's said.

"Well, guess what my next Purim costume is," Shira said. I had a feeling that what she was about to say was going to turn Purim, my favourite holiday of the year, into a personal nightmare. "I'm dressing up as Dragon Lady," Shira said.

It felt like my heart was clattering inside me. What if Esther found out? I'm sure she had no idea that the girls saw her as mean. It would be so embarrassing. What if Esther started wearing her necklace more often, I thought with rising panic. And what if Shira found a silly plastic elephant as part of her costume?

I shot a glance at my cell phone. I'd been trapped in there for four minutes but it felt like four epochs.

"That is brilliant," Natalie said, as all three of them burst out laughing. "Everyone at school is going to love it."

I clenched my fists. She was right. The entire student body would talk about Shira's horrible Dragon Lady costume for years to come.

"I'm going to the Salvation Army store, I swear I'm doing this, and I'm going to get an old lady outfit," Shira was saying, struggling to spit out the words through her laughter. "Then I'm going to stuff a pillow in my butt and another pillow down my top."

If this costume included the elephant necklace, the most private detail of Mrs. Levine's history would become the subject of knee-slapping hilarity on the graduation trip, year-end parties, and in yearbook signings.

"You should have heard her talking to Resnick," Natalie said. *"Oh, I hope you'll be focused, Raina. Because your life will be completely ruined and you'll end up homeless."*

"You know what my father told me?" Sarah said. "He's been at board meetings at ten o'clock at night and she's still in her office. That woman obviously has no life."

You have no idea.

"She's totally pathetic," Shira said. *"Girls, we care so very deeply about your development as individuals and students, we've decided to cancel all extracurricular activities, and keep you at school until ten at night so you can be as miserable as I am."*

Natalie chimed in on the fun. *"Misery is in the student handbook, girl. Have you read it again today?"*

I considered rising to Mrs. Levine's defence but decided that it was better not to incite the micro-mob here.

As an ex-Shira myself, I knew that all too well.

That night Professor K. and Esther got engaged.

The announcement on MazelTovNation was short on details. They were after all, three times as old as the typical couples on the site. I should have been happy, but what did it matter anymore? The *l'chaim* — a small and impromptu engagement party — was going to be held at the home of one of the board members of Moriah.

Dahlia hadn't been at school and her cell phone went straight to voicemail, and frankly this news was too important to text. I was still alone with this knowledge of Esther's identity.

At home, Leah wasn't making eye contact with me. She had told Matchmaven that she needed a break from dating, that she needed some time to recover from the humiliation and the pain of Jake. With Professor K. busy with Mrs. Levine, Tamara away, Leah cutting me off, and Dahlia sick, I felt completely lost. I was down to Bubby.

The worst thing of all was the nagging fear that Mr. Sacks might not make it.

The night of the *l'chaim*, I had to force myself to get dressed for a party. I had little desire to sit around with five senior citizens and discuss the upcoming wedding. I also didn't really know how to relate to Mrs. Levine/Esther anymore. On top of that, Leah was probably going to beat herself up over the fact that two seniors could find love but she couldn't.

While Aunt Mira and Leah finished dressing, I threw on a black pencil skirt and a maroon cardigan and trudged to the family room hoping to find Bubby.

Thankfully, she was watching a ball game, the voice of an unfamiliar announcer filling the room. *"It's a clear sky today at Citi Field. The temperature is a balmy seventy degrees in New York City."* The only image of New York my head could conjure right now was

Mr. Sacks lying in some random hospital there.

"It's just the Mets," Bubby said dismissively.

"I wish I was there," I said out loud.

Bubby glanced at me, and then turned back to the TV where the pitcher was releasing a cut fastball. Applause filled the stadium as the ball sailed past the batter. The catcher finally marched up to the mound and huddled with the pitcher. The batter wiggled his thighs and sliced the air with his bat a few times while he waited for the catcher to finish conferring with the pitcher.

Instead of improving my mood, the game just taunted me and stoked the ache that was in my heart.

The catcher was done now and he strode past home plate and crouched down on his haunches. A forkball came next and narrowly missed the bat, much to the crowd's delight. The camera then zoomed to the catcher, whose gloved hand stretched below his left knee while he quickly flicked out four fingers with the other.

"What a pain," I blurted out, helpless to the growing misery that was drowning me.

"What are you talking about?" Bubby said.

"Well, what if there's a runner on second?" I said. "He could *see* the catcher."

She threw up her hands in annoyance. "What's the matter with you? You know they always change the signals."

"Well, when you think about it, it's a lot of effort to go through when you could just communicate directly." What *was* the matter with me?

I shifted on the couch, uncomfortable in every position. We watched in silence for a few minutes, until Bubby turned to me.

"You know, Raina," she said in a quiet voice. "You don't always need to go to the mound."

I bit my lip.

She turned her gaze back to the TV. "We're probably going to leave soon anyway," she said.

I sprang up from the couch. "I'll be two minutes."

"Sure you will," she said. "I'll tell Mira you have the runs."

I bounded up the stairs to the bathroom, slammed the door behind me, then began searching for names of random hospitals in New York City. A force of energy overcame me as I started jotting down numbers. Maybe I could do a long-distance apology.

"Rain." Mira rapped on the door. "We're leaving in ten minutes. You okay?"

"Be right there," I said.

I searched for more phone numbers: Lennox Hill, Mount Sinai, and Columbia Presbyterian. I started calling. Mordechai Sacks wasn't at any of those hospitals.

No matter. I kept dialling until I was down to my last hospital when another loud knock jarred me.

"Raina!" It was Mira. "Uncle Eli and I are heading out to the car."

"One second," I said. The fact was that my work with Professor K. and Esther was done. None of it mattered.

My hand shook as I pressed the screen on the phone for my last hospital, New York General.

I ran the faucet so nobody could hear me talking. I dialled the number. I found him. It was like hitting cardiac jackpot at New York General Hospital.

Mr. Sacks was in the coronary care unit. "Can I please speak to Mordechai Sacks? This is his daughter." Spoken like the true liar that I'd become.

"Hold the line, please."

"Hello?" a woman said. "Can I help you?"

"Yes, my grandfather, Mordechai Sacks, is in the intensive care unit. Can I speak to him?"

"People in the unit don't usually have conversations," she said. "Who did you say you were?"

"I'm calling for my mother," I said. "Her father — my grandfather — is in the unit. Mordechai Sacks."

"Hang on," she said.

A male voice finally got on the line.

"Hello?"

"Is this . . . Mr. Sacks?" I said.

There was a pause. The sound of beeping could be heard in the background.

"Hello?" I repeated.

"Who is this?" the man said.

"It's Rain, Raina Resnick. I had sent Mr. Sacks a letter and I'd like to talk to him."

After another hesitation he finally spoke.

"I'm sorry to tell you this," he said. "But my great-uncle passed away a few hours ago."

My mouth opened, but no sound came out.

"His heart gave out in his sleep," he said. It felt like the air was being suctioned out of my lungs. And it hurt. It hurt so badly. I crossed my arms and hugged myself and dropped to the floor. But the floor wasn't low enough for me.

"Are you okay?" the man on the phone said. "Are you still there?"

I wiped my cheek with the back of my hand.

"I . . . I wanted to speak to him," I said. "I was his student.

It was me. He . . . he was fired. I . . ." Between the sobbing and hiccupping it was impossible to communicate. I inhaled a deep breath and let it out slowly.

"I was the one who sat down at the computer before he logged off his server," I said. "I sent those emails from his name. It was me that got him fired and then he got the heart condition and now he's —" My chest began heaving again.

"No, no, no. Please, stop." He actually chuckled. "I'm not sure who you are, but you did *not* kill my great uncle. Nor did you get him fired. He was supposed to retire a year and a half ago, but the school insisted that he stay on for another year."

"What?"

"He was doing them a favour the last year that he taught. And his heart condition? He's had that for years."

"But I embarrassed him," I said in a voice that seemed to come from a distant place.

"What's your name?"

"Raina Resnick."

"That name sounds familiar." I felt the back of my neck heat up.

"Wait, I know. I've been going through the stuff in his apartment the last few weeks. I just might have seen an envelope with your name on it, but there was no address. I've got three boxes full of papers in my van. I was just going to dump it all out. I sure wouldn't have known how to send it to you. Let me check."

"Please . . . do you think you could go down to your car and look for the envelope?"

"The funeral's in a couple of hours." I should have known that. The burial traditionally takes place as soon as possible.

"Oh," I said in a quivering voice.

"Obviously this is important to you and maybe this is something that Uncle Mordechai wanted taken care of before he was buried. Give me your phone and email address. If I find anything I'll mail —"

"No. Could you read it?"

"That urgent?" he said. "Fine. If you don't mind me looking. How about this, I'll read it to you and then mail it. Is that okay?"

"Thank you," I sobbed.

"Rain," Aunt Mira was yelling. "If you can't go just tell me but this is just plain rude. We have to go *now*."

"I have to go now," I whispered. "Can I ask your name?"

"Simon," he said. "I'll try to call you soon."

I wiped my eyes, opened the bathroom door, and descended the stairs behind her. Bubby had my coat in her hands and handed it to me. We walked into the biting winter night and I slipped into the seat next to Bubby with Leah following me. I put my phone on vibrate and held it, so I could answer immediately if Simon called.

Aunt Mira and Uncle Eli were chattering about how nice it was for one of the board members of Moriah to host the gathering tonight.

When we entered the house I gasped at the scene. The entire main floor was filled with people. The small *l'chaim* for five guests had turned into an engagement party worthy of Tamara and Jeremy. There had to be over a hundred people crammed into the main floor. Even though it was a mile away from the Bernsteins' house, it was the same model. The dining room table was covered with platters of bagels, lox, and cheeses, as well as pastries and fruit.

It was impossible to get through the crush of people so

I took a shortcut through the kitchen. A familiar face was there playing with two small children. He was tall — over six feet — with brown hair, brown eyes, and olive skin. He was twentysomething and wore black dress pants and a white button-down shirt.

"Ari! Again!" A little boy stretched his arms up to the tall man. "Again!"

Ari scooped up the boy and tossed him in the air with a laugh. I stood transfixed. I had seen him somewhere before.

"Me too, Ari!"

Ari gently put down the boy and picked up the tiny girl and raised her in the air. Both children squealed with delight.

"Ari," someone called out. "*Zayda* is going to speak now!"

Professor K.'s grandson! I had seen his photograph many times in Professor K.'s living room as well as in the photo album. Ari straightened himself up and patted the boy on the shoulder. "If there's time, I'll read you a story later," Ari said.

The front door slammed with yet more guests arriving. It was starting to feel like the Number 7 bus in here.

"Rain!" It was Aunt Mira. "Professor Kellman is waiting for you." Ari smiled at me.

I entered the living room and worked my way next to Bubby. I glanced back at the kitchen to see if I could check out Ari some more and noted Dahlia stood at the entrance, waving at me. Finally, she was better! I swiped a brownie off the table and held it up to Dahlia. We exchanged an understanding glance. The brownie was useless — it was *baked*, for heaven's sake.

Professor K. was speaking now. For just one minute I was going to try to enjoy their happiness. "I am so thrilled," he said. "I never dreamt I'd find this kind of happiness at this stage of my life."

Mira, who stood next to me, gave me a hug. "It's so wonderful, isn't it?"

"Esther Levine is my dream girl," Professor K. said, as he gazed lovingly at her. "Sometimes it's worth it to wait a long time for your soul mate."

I glanced around the table. The last thing Leah needed was to hear a seventy-five-year-old celebrate that he finally met his soul mate. She stood at the edge of the table with a bagel on her plate, but didn't seem to be reacting at all.

I took a bite out of the brownie as Professor K. continued his speech. "And it never, ever would have happened without the efforts of a very special person."

I stopped chewing.

"And I need to express gratitude to that wonderful person."

My heart hammered inside me. Was he about to thank me, or the anonymous email account?

"Matchmaven!" he practically shouted.

So that was it. I squeezed my eyes shut.

"Let's all raise our glasses to Matchmaven," he said.

I could feel beads of sweat form on my forehead as everyone shouted *"l'chaim!"* How long does it take to thank someone anonymous? Couldn't he start praising his bride already?

Professor K. smiled at Mrs. Levine. "Here's to our good luck."

It looked like he was moving on.

"That wasn't just luck," an indignant Bubby said in a booming voice. "It was plenty hard work." An uncomfortable silence filled the air. Bubby apparently had decided to take over the engagement party. Leah was visibly cringing now. Where was

Bubby going with this anyway? A queasy feeling sloshed inside my stomach.

"Bubby," I whispered. "Let's just let Professor Kellman give his speech."

"What do you mean, Ma?" Uncle Eli said.

"Bubby, you're interrupting," I hissed at Bubby.

"Raina," Professor K. said. "Let's hear what Mrs. Bernstein has to say."

"So who exactly is this Matchmaven, Bayla?" a familiar voice yelled out. "You sound like you know!"

I froze.

"Never mind," Bubby said, sniffing.

Mrs. Feldman wagged her finger at Bubby. "You have to be an expert on everything, Bayla."

"Look who's talking, Sylvia." Bubby snorted.

I couldn't believe it. They were actually going to have a fight in the middle of the engagement party.

I glanced at Uncle Eli whose eyebrows were drawn together. Mira had a look of terror on her face. You'd think that when you lived with Bubby you'd be used to it, but apparently you had to be constantly vigilant about avoiding a scene.

"Okay, Bayla, big talker," Mrs. Feldman said. "Tell us who it is."

I dropped my eyes to my hand; it was clenched so tightly, that the brownie was all crumbs now. A hush settled on the crowd, and all eyes rested on Bubby.

"If you knew who it was, you'd stop pretending that you knew and would just say who it is," Mrs. Feldman said.

The logic escaped me, but it was Bubby that I was terrified about. They were goading her to give up the goods.

"I'll just say that she's very young and very caring." Bubby turned to me and smiled sweetly.

My entire body began to tremble.

"What are you saying, Ma?" Mira's face was wound tight like a coil.

"Never mind," Bubby said. "Leah, pass me some chocolate, why don't you. Those deviled eggs look delicious too."

I could have kissed Bubby. The danger was over, right? Through the side of my eye, Leah looked like she was about to cry.

"Ma?" Eli said. Leah's eyes were bulging out of her head now.

Over at the entrance to the kitchen, Dahlia had a look of panic on her face.

I bit my lip and willed Bubby to keep her mouth closed. But the limelight was too irresistible. I grabbed Bubby's arm and whispered, "Bubby, please."

"Don't be rude, Raina," Mrs. Feldman said. "Let her speak."

I swallowed.

"Fine," Bubby said. "Why can't we give thanks where it's due." She turned to me and took my hand. "Mira, you give her such a hard time but you should be *proud* of this girl. She does nothing but devote her life to helping other people. She spends every single waking minute trying to bring happiness to all kinds of people. Why can't you see how special she is?"

"What are you saying, Mrs. Bernstein?" Mrs. Levine said, her face tight.

"You want to know what I'm saying?" Bubby said. "I'm *saying*, that our own Raina Resnick is Matchmaven."

First there was silence.

Then a loud smashing sound broke the quiet as Leah's plate fell out of her hands and clattered to the floor. The room started spinning. Air sucked out of my lungs. I couldn't breathe. Finally someone spoke. "What are you talking about?" Mrs. Feldman said with a snort. "Raina is a *child*."

"Raina?" Mira said, her eyes wide with shock. "Of course this isn't true, right?"

A jumble of disbelieving comments volleyed through the air.

Leah's face was frozen. I felt like I was going to pass out.

At that moment there was only one place I wanted to be.

Hong Kong.

Seriously. I wanted to be far away from Leah, and Mira, and Mrs. Levine, and all the disappointment they were feeling now — and Hong Kong never looked as delectably appealing as it did right now.

"Rain?" Professor K. said, as he peered at me intently. "Are you really Matchmaven?"

I gulped. The room was so silent you could feel the hum of the refrigerator.

I took a deep breath.

"Yes. It's true," I said weakly. "I'm Matchmaven."

Mrs. Levine gasped and her eyes watered.

Professor K. clapped his hands together and laughed. "That's wonderful! You come up here, young lady," he said.

I shook my head and backed away. "No, no, no."

"Come on, Rain. I insist. Don't be so modest."

Leah's eyes were two cluster bombs of shock now.

"Come on, Rain," Professor K. said. "Everyone wants you to say a few words." I was the focal point of the room. I inched toward him. Mrs. Levine's gaze dropped to the floor, unable to meet my eyes.

Safe within his matrimonial bubble, Professor K. was completely oblivious to the disbelief that circulated the room.

"I'm delighted that it's you, Raina." Professor K. addressed the gathering. "This girl is a bright, caring, and special young lady and Esther and I owe her a huge debt of gratitude. Come on now, Raina."

He turned his eyes on me and waited. I stumbled up to Professor K. and stood between him and Mrs. Levine. Mrs. Levine was desperately trying to smile, but her eyes were wide with shock. Was that shame I read on her cheeks? Anger? Meanwhile, Leah was turning varying shades of red. I gulped and took a deep breath.

"I just wanted to say *mazel tov* to Professor Kellman and Mrs. Levine. When I see the two of you I feel that you were meant to be together. And . . . if I hadn't done it, someone else would. So I wish you the best of luck for a lifetime of joy." I shrugged and turned to flee the room.

"But Rain, how on earth did this happen?" Uncle Eli said.

"We want to hear!" It was Mrs. Feldman.

Leah shook her head at me. Her face was a kaleidoscope of shock, hurt, and anger. She looked like she couldn't breathe properly.

"Come on, everyone's waiting," Professor K. said. Then he leaned over and whispered in my ear. "Have you met my grandson? Maybe you have a girl for him?"

He clapped his hands. "Okay, everyone. Our matchmaker will now speak."

I took a deep breath and started talking. At this point there was nothing more to lose.

"I became a matchmaker accidentally, and against my will." That was met with a lot of raised eyebrows.

"It all started on the bus to school in a strange city where I didn't know anybody. I met this sweet woman who begged me to fix her up. I'm sixteen years old. What do I know about matchmaking? I only knew one eligible man in the city and this woman was so desperate for a husband, and I was so desperate for a friend. So I fixed them up."

My eyes pleaded with Leah now, because she was the one I was talking to. Her face remained motionless.

"I didn't know that he was supposed to go out with my sister. I was so scared when I found out that I couldn't tell anybody.

"The match worked out, and she raved to a friend. Word spread and I was soon inundated with matchmaking requests by people who had just given up. Given up on matchmakers. Given up on meeting people on their own. Given up on online dating. People who had resigned themselves to a life of loneliness." I sighed.

The guests were silent again. *Please Leah, don't hate me.*

"I was going to send out emails explaining that this was all a mistake. I'm no matchmaker. But then I got an email from my sister.

"I so badly wanted to help her so I did a practice match with others before attempting to fix her up. But when it didn't work out, they each asked me to find someone else for them. It kept growing and multiplying. And the more I realized how much pain these people were feeling, the more difficult it became to turn them away. It takes so much time to make a match, and to talk to people, and listen to their concerns. And sometimes you're pleading with some single to give another person a second chance and other times you're practically cutting a deal to get them to go on another date. But you're always sharing their sadness and frustration with them. In the end though? I did it for one reason. For my sister, Leah. I tried so hard. I know that I didn't succeed for Leah but everything I did was for her."

I looked at Leah; my gaze was loaded with pleading and regret.

"Professor K. is my friend," I said turning to Mrs. Levine. Her arms were crossed and she was doing a heroic attempt at a smile.

"I didn't know who Esther was. She never gave me a last name, but she was so kind and intelligent. I loved our emails. I felt like she could understand things that nobody else could."

Her face relaxed and she nodded slightly.

"The matches literally took up all my time. Sometimes our perceptions of people can be so distorted, you know? I was like so many people I fix up and couldn't get past the stupid image thing," I said, thinking of how I used to perceive Mr. Sacks. How I used to perceive everyone, really.

I hadn't intended on talking about Esther but once I got going it was impossible to stop. My story just spilled out of me. It felt amazing. I hadn't even ever told Dahlia the whole thing. It was a Mrs. Marmor moment. Or hour. I suddenly understood why people went on *Oprah* and completely exposed themselves. It just felt so darned good.

"I started tanking at school because of it. All my spare time was devoted to making matches. How could I turn away? They needed me. But with Esther and Professor K. — it seemed like a natural match," I said. "I've done some not-so-nice things in the past. So maybe I deserve to have a lot of people upset with me. But their happiness is all that matters. Thank you."

The room was silent. No one seemed to know what to do next.

Mrs. Levine observed me. "Rain," she finally said. I braced myself. This was the moment I had feared more than anything else.

"Please, please forgive me," I babbled. "I promise you I didn't know it was you. I just wanted to help. All I knew is that I loved your emails and I knew that you and Professor K. would be soul mates."

"Rain," she said quietly. "Give me a hug." Mrs. Levine leaned over and wrapped me in her arms and the room erupted in applause. "Thank you, darling," she whispered in my ear.

Mrs. Levine released me as Bubby and Mira appeared next to her.

"I'm so sorry, Aunt Mira."

Mira shook her head. "Rain, this whole thing is crazy. I can't believe I didn't know this was going on the whole time."

Bubby was smirking. "What's the matter with you?"

"How did you know, Bubby?" I said.

"You think I'd ever sleep through an episode of *Mod Squad*?" Bubby said. "Do you see what Linc looked like? Of course I knew what she was doing on the computer every night."

I shook my head, but a tiny twinge prickled me. "But Bubby, why did you out me?"

"Because I couldn't stand it anymore," she said. "It was making me crazy already. Everyone blamed you all the time when they should have been *thanking* you."

"But we didn't know," Mira said.

"It's true," Mrs. Levine said. "I'm so sorry that you had the weight of this on your own."

Bubby was not about to let anyone off the hook. "This girl devoted every spare minute to helping other people," she said in an accusing voice. "And all she got was blame, *Mira*."

Mira's face fell. "I'm so sorry I couldn't be there for you," she said.

"But *I* was there for her," Bubby said, throwing her arm around my shoulder.

Mira looked at both of us. "You two are cut from the same cloth."

"Well, speaking of cloth, I ordered two Red Sox sweaters for us," Bubby said to me. "And this summer when the Sox come to Toronto I'm taking you to a ball game."

"I'm in!"

Bubby leaned over and whispered into my ear. "And we're going to get hot dogs. *Lots* of hot dogs."

Dahlia was shaking her head in disbelief at the entrance to the kitchen.

I tripped out of the dining room and into the kitchen where Dahlia now stood next to the kitchen counter, her iPad open in front of her. "This is the *craziest* night of my life. I cannot *believe* Esther was Mrs. Levine."

"Is that *wild*?" I said.

She laughed. "You must have had your heart attack already, because I'm still having mine now."

"Rain." It was Leah standing next to me. Her eyes glistened.

Dahlia returned to her iPad.

"Leah, I'm so sorry," I said. "I . . . just wanted to fix things. I wanted to find you a husband. I wanted you to not hate me anymore. I love you so much."

"Rain," she said softly. "It's okay."

"Really?"

"Really." She opened her arms and I flew into them. We hugged each other, rocking back and forth.

"I missed you so much," I said.

"Me too," Leah said. "Now I know why I liked Matchmaven so much!"

Dahlia gasped. "I don't believe this," she said. "You guys better look at this."

Dahlia was gaping at the computer. Leah and I peered over her shoulder where MazelTovNation was open.

News of the most recent announcements was on the top of the home page.

Ben was engaged. Leah's ex-fiancé.

"Mazel tov, Ben and Gila. You two were obviously so in love when I saw you at the Fourth of July barbecue at the Steins' house in San Diego. May you have a lifetime of joy."

Leah gasped.

Ben was dating Gila when he was still engaged to Leah.

No one said a word. Leah's face was white.

"You were right about him disappearing for the barbecue, Rain," she said in a shaking voice. "It was all just an excuse. Ben used it as an excuse to break up with me."

"I hate that I was right," I said.

She squeezed her eyes shut, her lips quivering.

I wrapped her in a hug.

"I feel like I should apologize to you," she said. "Ben wasn't honest with me and I shut you out. It was easier to blame you than to face the truth about him and our relationship."

"I just missed you so much," I said. "I would have done anything to win you back."

She let out a laugh through her tears. "*Anything* can be pretty scary with you, sis, so I'm glad you've been outed."

She yanked a tissue from her pocket and dabbed her eyes. "You never trusted Ben, did you?"

"No. And Jake too — although I did hope."

"You're pretty smart," Leah said. The reality of her love life must have suddenly hit her. "My makeup's running," she said, then fled to the bathroom.

"What a jerk that Ben is," Dahlia said, still gazing at the computer. "You know how to spot them."

"It's a gift."

But I felt a flash of anger because being right felt pretty awful. I seemed to be able to sniff out untrustworthy men the way Bronx could smell chocolate.

"I went to camp with him," a man's voice said. I spun around. It was Ari — Professor K.'s grandson. He peered over my other shoulder at the Ben–Gila announcement.

"He was . . . engaged to my sister then," I said as I pointed to the posting about the Fourth of July weekend.

"Hmmm." Ari nodded. "I guess your sister's better off."

"Definitely," Dahlia mumbled.

Ari held up his hands like he would say no more. He was obviously that kind of guy.

"Thank you so much for bringing my grandfather happiness," he said. "I'm very, very impressed with what you've done. You have spunk!"

"I've overdosed on spunk — I think that's my problem."

"Hey, here's my card," he said with a shy smile. "It sounds like you did a great job with my grandfather. Maybe you'll have me in mind too?"

"I do, already," I said with a smile. "I think I might have someone right here, as a matter of fact."

"Already?"

"Yup." I glanced at the powder room door that was still closed. I turned to Ari. "Can you come back in exactly ten minutes?"

"No problem," he said. "I'll be here!" He drifted back to his grandfather just as my phone rang — with an unrecognizable area code.

I answered it after the first ring. "It's Mr. Sack's great-nephew," I whispered to Dahlia.

"Put it on speaker," she said, gesturing to the phone.

"Is this Rain?" he asked. "It's Simon Sacks, Mordechai's great nephew. I found the letter."

Dear Raina,

I'm sorry I didn't respond to your letters earlier. I haven't been feeling too well.

I appreciate that you took the effort to write me twice. Please don't worry yourself about what happened last June. I have to admit, I wasn't in top form in my last year of teaching and yes, my memory is going. My health had deteriorated so badly, and nothing's been the same for me since my wife died.

We all knew that you have natural leadership skills and it was clear that you enjoyed being the centre of attention. But you're also bright, and if you would have applied yourself even a tiny bit you would have achieved more in school.

About that email, I realize that it was meant as a joke for your friends Maya and Danielle. But you can imagine how embarrassing it was when Rabbi Singer received a letter stating that due to increasing memory loss and depression I would no longer be able to teach and would use my time to travel to Reno and take up blackjack and cake decorating. I knew that I was becoming more absent-minded and that's why I wanted to retire, but I have to admit that it was painful to read the email and how you pointed out my lapses.

Nonetheless, I felt that it was wrong that you were asked to leave the school. I argued with Rabbi Singer that it was too drastic a measure, especially because we had heard from your family that you'd have to leave New York. I felt that rather than counselling you out, more could have been accomplished by working with you and supporting you. Judging by your letters, however, it sounds like you've done a lot of growing up in Toronto. I'm really glad to know that things worked out for you there and that it ended up being a positive opportunity for growth and change.

Raina, I've also made mistakes in my life and I've hurt people too. That's why I'm completely forgiving you. It sounds like you've really turned yourself around.

Raina, I wish you all the success and happiness that life can offer. And I hope that all of those tremendous talents that you have will be used to help other people. Yours truly,

Mordechai Sacks

I thanked Mr. Sacks's nephew and said goodbye.

I swallowed and bit my lip. Dahlia hugged me. Heat scalded the inside of my head and neck. My self-serving apology had not really earned this kindness. How could I have not recognized the man's generosity? I should have gotten to know him.

Leah returned from the bathroom, her mascara freshly applied. "I need you to know that Mr. Sacks sent me a letter," I said. "He said I wasn't to blame for his troubles. It's going to be mailed to me. I'll show it to you when I get it."

"No more apologizing, Rain," she said. "You're the one who deserves the apologies now."

"Let's call it even," I said.

"Now will you find me a guy?"

"Actually, Leah, I think I found him right here," I said. "And my gut trusts this one."

"Really?!" she said.

"Really."

She grinned at me. "Does this one like heels and makeup or no heels and makeup?"

"This one," I said, "doesn't care."

chapter 31

≫⟶ 100 Times Higher and 1,000 Times Lighter ⟵≪

The band was on fire.

We danced until our feet ached and our dresses clung to our bodies with sweat. Professor K. and Mrs. Levine had been married for a month now and couldn't keep their eyes off each other. They were as newlywedy as it comes. Mrs. Levine glowed with joy. She even let me help her choose a new wardrobe, which included shoes that didn't have a buckle or laces, and a looser hairstyle that she admitted made her feel more youthful. The only downside was something I'm not going to make a big deal about, but I'll just say two words and you'll understand.

Shoulder pads.

But today was Leah and Ari's day. She wore an elegant gown

inspired by an Alexander McQueen design. With her hair pinned up, framing her bright blue eyes, she was breathtaking. The truth is, though, that it was hard to notice anything but the happiness that charged through her body, loosened her limbs, and lit up her face.

Leah and Ari were bouncing on chairs raised in the air, as circles of revellers surrounded them. They were a cloth napkin away from each other, clutching each end of it, their eyes locked in a visual embrace. The men finally lowered the chairs to the ground and the women grabbed Leah.

She was immediately surrounded by concentric circles of dancers. Tamara, my mother, Aunt Mira, Mrs. Levine, Dahlia, and me joined together with clasped hands, driven by the music of the band. Even Bubby joined the circle, grasping my hand like she was never going to let go.

Leah pivoted until she saw me. She held out her hands and beckoned for me to join her at the centre. We locked arms, swayed from side to side, and grinned at each other. We were surrounded by members of my newly enlarged team of matchmakers. Mira, my mother, Leah, Bubby, and I were now all partners in the reformulated Matchmavens, Inc. — a group effort that would also be receiving extensive tech support from our webmaster Dahlia, who had almost completed construction of the official Matchmavens website.

The next few months would be busy ones. Deb was getting married and the Matchmaven Team — man, how I loved that word "team" — had a lot of follow-up work to do with our singles. Mira and Mom entered our circle and we gripped each other with laughter and song. It felt like I was bouncing on the bed in matchmaking flight, but a hundred times higher and a thousand times lighter.

acknowledgements

I am deeply grateful to Jack David who made this all happen, and in the most supportive way possible. The entire ECW Press team has been nothing short of awesome: Crissy Calhoun, Erin Creasey, Rachel Ironstone, Jenna Illies, and Michelle Melski. Special thanks to Jack for the gift of Kathy Lowinger. I am very, very fortunate to have worked with Crissy and Kathy, editorial goddesses, both.

Many thanks to my readers for their significant insight, feedback, and encouragement: Rowan Greene, Sharon Hart-Green, Natalie Hyde, Deborah Kerbel, Deena Nataf, Joseph Palumbo, and Sarah Zinman. Thanks to Marsha Skrypuch for her wisdom and for making the ultimate match. Thank you to the Ontario Arts Council for its generous support. Special thanks also go to my agent Claire Gerus, to my dear friend Allan Robbins, and to my father; I truly appreciate all their help, ideas, and support. And for their inspiration: David, Orit, Michael, Merav, Techiya, Kaylee, Shalvi, and Aliza. And thank you thank you (yes, I wrote that twice) Marty. Rain would never have been born without you.